On
Carrick
Shore

On Carrick Shore

ALEX J. WRIGHT

THE CHOIR PRESS

First published in the United Kingdom in 2018 by
The Choir Press

ISBN 978-1-911589-57-0

Contents

————

Dedication

———

For Andy and Simon, and in memory of my grandparents, Bob and Jean Dalziel.

Acknowledgements

———

Grateful thanks for their help and encouragement to Gordon and Lesley Wright, Alice Mayoux and Theresa Sowerby.

Thanks also to Miles, Rachel and Adrian at The Choir Press for their advice and practical help.

CHAPTER 1

Monday July 30th 1781

"Bloody Ailsa Craig," he muttered. "I thought I'd seen the last o' ye."

From the top of the rise, the rider surveyed the scene before him. In the mild early afternoon sunshine the rigs of green barley sloped down towards the sea, the gulls wheeling and squawking in the still air. The waters of the Firth of Clyde were calm, the surface like green-blue silk shot through with lighter and darker shades above the lazy currents. He could see the blue hills of Arran and behind, the low hazy outline of the Mull of Kintyre. To his left, offshore, rose the sheer cliffs and perfectly conical top of the vast rock which haunted the dreams of every exiled Carrick man.

He wheeled his horse round and set off reluctantly towards Ayr, to face the wrath of his father.

*

Thomas Boyd, twenty years old, graduate of the University of Glasgow, was going home after two years in Paris, where he had served an apprenticeship with the prosperous wine merchant Alphonse Lefèvre. This post had been procured for him by his father, Sir Malcolm Boyd, who had serious doubts about his second son's ability to make his way in the world, and preferred him to make that way as far from Ayr as possible.

Somewhat against expectations, Tom had proved to be a quick learner with an agile mind and a good deal of initiative, but just as his employer was about to offer him a permanent position, disaster struck and he was dismissed in disgrace. Lacking the means to support himself in France, a country still at war with his own, his only solution was to return to

Scotland. The journey had been long and weary, and he had no doubt that his reception would not be warm.

*

An hour later, Tom clattered into the stable yard of Barnessie House, scattering hens and geese as he went, and slowly dismounted. Any joy he felt at seeing his old home again was overlaid with the dread of facing his family.

"Aye, it's yersel'" said a voice, "It's guid tae see ye." Tom turned to see the grinning face of Bob Balfour, his father's groom and a friend from childhood. A short wiry man of twenty-six with a big nose and slightly bandy legs, Bob came into his own on horseback. He also seemed to have shrunk in the two years since Tom had last seen him.

"Man, ye've fair grown," said Bob, clasping Tom's arm affectionately, "and ye've no' turned oot sae bad. Nae wonder the lassies is a' efter ye."

"It's guid tae see ye, Bob," said Tom hurriedly. "How are ye keeping? And Jeanie? Nae bairns yet?"

"Och, we've time enough. Jeanie's in the kitchen. Awa' ye go ben, seeing you're no' minded tae gang roun' tae the front door. I'll see tae yer horse. She looks fair wabbit an' a'," he added, stroking the mare's flanks.

Tom crossed the yard and entered the kitchen, where Bob's wife was rolling pastry while supervising the work of two kitchen maids.

"They've ca'd for tea upstairs," she was saying, "and Sir Malcolm's no' in the best o' moods, so mind ye dinnae cowp onything. Tak the shortbread and the scones, and serve it on the guid china." She broke off when she caught sight of Tom.

"Aye, it's yersel'" she said, repeating the words of her husband in a somewhat different tone, "the prodigal son." A plump, fair-haired young woman, Jeanie had a sharp tongue and a clear idea of her place in the world, which was the equal of anyone, high or low, and of her right to speak her mind. "Ye've a bit o' a nerve coming back here efter a' the trouble ye've caused. Is that no' right, Bob?" she added as her husband entered the kitchen. Bob grunted but offered no opinion.

Tom coloured and quickly withdrew his hand, which had been straying towards a tempting pile of apple slices on the table. Suddenly he was tired, hungry and sorry for himself. He resolved to get whatever was coming to him over with as soon as possible and turned towards the door leading to the front stairs. Jeanie's voice rang in his ears.

"Aye, awa' ben the hoose. Whaur dae ye think *you're* going, Bob? I need ye tae rise this pie shell. Ye're better at it nor me, but wash yer hands first."

Tom made his way up the handsome staircase to the first floor, past the row of portraits of his forebears, censorious to a man. Why did they all have to look so accusing, so like his father?

*

Sir Malcolm Boyd was taking tea with his wife Margaret, his elder son David and his twelve-year-old daughter Kate in the well-proportioned family parlour of the house he had had built ten years previously. Barnessie House was a testament to the prosperity he enjoyed as a landowner and one of the leading lawyers of his day. The large windows looked out over green lawns to the stand of beech and rowan trees and beyond to the enclosed fields farmed by David. He reflected that life had been good to him; he had a loving wife, a fine, upstanding son who would inherit his estate and a lively daughter who would no doubt make a good marriage or care for her parents in their old age, or both. He had worked hard for his position in life and intended to enjoy it. The only fly in the ointment was his second son, whose arrival was expected in a few days' time and who would be dealt with severely.

He was about to take another sip of tea when a noise on the landing made him look up. There, framed in the doorway, stood his younger son, a sheepish expression on his face.

"Guid day faither, mither," said Tom.

The teacup rattled in the saucer and tea was spilt all over the tray as Sir Malcolm leapt to his feet, incandescent with rage.

"It's you, ye skellum," he roared, "the ne'er-dae-weel that cannae keep his pintle in his breeks!"

There was a nervous giggle from Kate, quickly hushed by her mother. "Go to your room, Kate" said Lady Margaret.

Kate left the room slowly, with an inquisitive stare at Tom as she passed him. She only went as far as the landing, where she settled down on the floor by the door to listen.

"What hae ye got tae say for yersel'?" asked Sir Malcolm in a deceptively quiet voice, "after ye've lost a' yer prospects and made me the laughing stock o' Ayr?"

"Sorry, faither," mumbled Tom.

"Sorry?" roared his sire. "I'll gie ye sorry. I've a mind tae hang ye up by the lugs and use yer baw-bags for golf balls!"

Lady Margaret looked down, embarrassed; David studied the scene beyond the window and outside the door Kate's eyes widened in a mixture of horror and glee.

"Better gowf ba's than the use ye've made o' them, it seems," went on Sir Malcolm. "I sent ye tae France tae learn a respectable trade, no' tae mak free wi' yer employer's daughter an' lose yer guid name."

"But faither, nothing happened, I ..."

"Nothing?" roared his father. "I've had a letter frae M. Lefèvre. Dae ye deny ye were found in bed wi' the dochter, what's her name, Madeleine?"

At the mention of her name, Tom had a vision of golden hair, laughing blue eyes and a pert smile he had been powerless to resist. He sighed.

"I cannae deny it," he said. "But nothing actually happened. We didnae ..."

"Just as weel ye were caught in time. It's bad enough that ye've lost yer reputation and near ruined the lassie, withoot an unwanted bairn."

"She's no' ruined," protested Tom. "Madeleine's family are

standing by her. They've said nothing; she's just gaun tae her aunt's in the country for a month. No' like here – it seems a'body kens aboot it. Jeanie ca'd me a prodigal son."

"Ye've yer aunties tae thank for that," said Sir Malcolm bitterly, with a glance at his wife. "Yon pair o' bletherin' beldames hae spread the news a' ower the toon. I ken they're yer sisters, Margaret, but I'd pit them baith in scold's bridles if it wasnae ower guid for them. As for "standin' by ye", what dae ye expect me tae dae, ye skellum?"

There followed a seemingly never-ending tirade in which the words poltroon, wastrel, cuif, glaikit sumph and fushionless gowk recurred frequently. Delivered with the full force of Sir Malcolm's powerful lungs, it could be heard throughout the house and penetrated as far as the kitchen, where Bob and Jeanie paused in the construction of the pie. "Weel, he's in guid voice," opined Jeanie. "I nearly feel sorry for the laddie."

"Dae ye think we should dae something?" asked Bob.

"I think he's near finished. It's quieter noo."

And sure enough, an ominous silence fell.

Upstairs, as her husband ran out of steam at last, Lady Margaret crossed the room and reached up to embrace the prodigal. "Welcome hame, son," she said. David too, came to clasp his brother's shoulder affectionately, and Tom felt tears gather behind his eyelids. On the landing, Kate breathed a sigh of relief.

But Sir Malcolm hadn't quite finished with Tom yet. In a deceptively quiet voice he asked, "What are ye gaun' tae dae for money? I suppose ye've nane left."

"No, faither," said Tom shamefacedly. "I spent the last in London, on Sadie."

"Sadie?" roared his father. "Wha in the name o' the wee man is Sadie? Anither jade?"

"No, faither. Sadie's my horse."

David's loud guffaw almost drowned a delighted giggle from the landing.

"Humph," said Sir Malcolm, but there was a gleam of reluctant amusement in his eye. "Aye, weel, I'll no' turn ye awa' frae the door. Ye can bide here for the time being, but ye'll need tae mak yersel' useful, mind. There's some tea left in the pot."

CHAPTER 2

Tuesday August 7th 1781

Useful. During the following week, Tom tried his best. He went to the fields with David, but had little aptitude or inclination for the work. He hung around the kitchen till Jeanie rapped his fingers with her wooden spoon, declaring he'd pinched one piece of pie-bound fruit too many, and sent him outside. In the stables Bob, when offered assistance, replied "No' just the noo, maybe later," until Tom didn't ask any more.

He missed Madeleine. She had befriended him during his first anxious days as an apprentice in her father's business, when no-one seemed to care about an awkward lad from Scotland with gauche manners and limited French. Madeleine had asked him about his home and family, introduced him to her friends and, although she teased and provoked him, had educated him in the ways of polite French society. As a result he had fallen in love for the first time, and his enforced parting from Madeleine had hit him hard.

As the days passed, time hung heavy on his hands. His only occupations seemed to be teaching Kate, a willing pupil, the kind of French not found in her school books, and riding around the lanes and fields and through the woods down to the shore, to watch the shifting moods of the sea and count the waves breaking on the shingle beach. He sometimes ventured into Ayr, but too many people in the cramped, bustling streets knew his story and he had to put up with knowing looks, scornful laughter or, in the case of church elders and pious matrons, a visible drawing aside of coats and skirts. His young adventurous spirit chafed at the confines of this small town and he longed to be back in Paris where everywhere new ideas were being discussed and the air was charged with a coming storm.

After a week or so, his mother sent him into Ayr to call on her sisters, the Misses McFadzean. "They're keen tae see you."

"Aye, they just want some mair tae gossip aboot."

"What's done's done," said his mother. "They cannae help gossiping, whiles, an' they mean nae harm. Be polite tae them, and mak' yourself useful."

"Useful, aye useful," he grumbled as he set off. "How can folk no' just be pleased to see me?"

The Misses McFadzean, spinster ladies approaching forty, occupied a handsome house in the Sandgate, home to those of the gentry of Ayr who had not yet moved to the country and to such fashionable shops as could be found in a small but increasingly prosperous town. The broad airy street contrasted with the noisy bustle of the High Street with its fish market, stinking gutters and smoky taverns.

The maid showed Tom into the first-floor parlour where Miss Letitia and Miss Euphemia McFadzean were enthroned, each in a delicate silk-upholstered chair on either side of a neat square window which afforded them a view of the ever-shifting panorama of the street and its attendant sources of gossip. A substantial sum inherited from their father enabled them to live in comfortable idleness, some compensation for the passing years and their dwindling hopes of a good marriage such as their elder sister Margaret had made.

Tom stood uncertainly on the threshold for a moment, dazzled partly by the sunshine coming through the window but more by the colours in the room. The walls were hung with a bright yellow paper on which exotic birds of every hue perched in a painted jungle of acid green. His aunts were equally colourfully decked out in satin dresses, Miss Euphemia in puce and Miss Letitia in green, each trimmed with a complicated arrangement of lace and ribbons.

Tom blinked, sketched an awkward bow and advanced into the room.

"Ah, the prodigal son," squawked Miss Euphemia. (*How many more times?* thought Tom wearily.) "Come awa' in and tell us aboot Paris. Is it as fashionable as they say?"

Thinking that he had certainly seen nothing in Paris to compare with the monstrosities his aunts were wearing, Tom perched warily on the edge of a fragile embroidered chair which creaked alarmingly under his weight, wondering how soon he could decently make his escape.

"Did ye go to court?" asked Miss Letitia eagerly. "Did ye see the Queen?"

"Is she as elegant as they say?" chimed in her sister.

Tom sighed. How could he explain that the Versailles court was a closed world which he could never enter; few did. That his knowledge of Paris came from frequenting clubs and coffee houses, mixing with young lawyers and journalists who belonged to a very different France, and hearing their heated discussions of a future which did not include the hated aristocracy symbolised by Louis XVI and his wife Marie-Antoinette, l'Autrichienne.

"I'm afraid I've never seen the Queen, or the King," he said.

"But ye were in Paris!" cried Miss Letitia. "That's where they live, is it no'?"

"No' exactly," said Tom. "They live at Versailles, that's like from here to Maybole, but they dinnae gang oot much."

"Oh." Miss Letitia was visibly disappointed. "But you must hae seen some wonderful things in Paris."

Yes, he had, thought Tom. There was Madeleine, for a start. He could not talk of her to his family, nor could he explain to his aunts the excitement he had felt in the teeming streets, the turmoil of new ideas discussed in crowded coffee houses, the feeling of being at the centre of an old world on the brink of change. He glanced out of the window at the sedate progress of horses and carts in the Sandgate, accompanied by the persistent squawking of seagulls, and wondered for the hundredth time if these were the limits of his horizons now. He blinked and realised that he himself was now the subject of the conversation.

"It's Malcolm I feel sorry for," Miss Euphemia was saying with a certain relish. "Spending a' that money tae send the young pup abroad and getting nae thanks for it."

"Getting mair like a slap in the face," opined her sister.

"It's a slur on the guid name o' a' the family."

"Aye, I'm feart tae show my face in decent society noo."

"Never mind at the kirk."

"And the young wastrel doesnae seem the least bit sorry."

The young wastrel coughed politely.

"Aunt Effie, Aunt Letty, it's been a pleasure, but I really must be awa' noo." Then he remembered the reason for his visit. "That is, unless I can be useful in ony way."

The two aunts tilted their heads and exchanged a look (*a pre-arranged signal*, Tom thought).

"Weel, if it's no' too much trouble ..." said Effie.

"... too great a call on your precious time ..." continued Letty.

"... seeing that we cannae show oor faces in the street ..."

"... prisoners in oor ain hame ..." sighed Letty.

"... You could go a wee message for us."

"Anything" said Tom, a little too hastily.

"You can fetch the lace we ordered frae Fleming the draper."

*

"Faither's got his sums wrong again."

Alison Fleming tutted affectionately, standing at the desk in the back shop of her father's tailor's and draper's business in the Sandgate, adding up the columns of figures as she checked the accounts. Her father had seen to it that she had a good education and, recognising early on her skill with a needle and head for figures, brought her up to be his creative and business associate, his partner in all but name. Alison loved the freedom he gave her to design and make clothes, as well as her involvement in the buying of cloth and the financial side of the business. It had flourished in recent years, allowing them to move from Irvine to new modern premises in the Sandgate. She particularly enjoyed making outfits for the wealthy ladies of Ayr and trying to introduce them to new fashion trends. For all that, she had a vague feeling that life had perhaps more to offer and that she would soon be twenty-one and had never been further than Kilmarnock.

The sound of the front door opening brought her mind back to the present, and a muffled thud and muttered curse sent her rushing through to the shop, where she found her father's new tailor's dummy lying on its side and a tall, angry-looking young man with floppy black hair standing over it. She noticed that his fine blue coat was the exact shade of his eyes and had obviously not been made in Scotland.

"What dae ye leave thon thing standing in the way for, where onybody could cowp it?" he demanded.

Alison forbore to point out that "thon thing" was essential to their business and had cost her father a pretty penny. She moved to set it upright and remove it from harm's way. "Can I help ye, sir?" she asked smoothly.

"I was told tae fetch lace here for my aunts," said the young man, not very graciously.

"Ah, that would be the Misses McFadzean. You must be Master Tom."

"How dae ye ken that?" demanded Tom suspiciously. This girl had no doubt heard the gossip and was making fun of him. Yet he could find no trace of mockery in her fine-boned face and clear grey eyes.

"I hae lace on order for two ladies called McFadzean and I've heard them talk aboot their nephew Tom, that's all. Oh, and your coat looks Parisian," she added, bending to open a drawer.

Tom looked round the shop, at the colourful displays of ribbons and lace and the shelves stacked with fabric of every kind, from flannel and linen to woven wool and broadcloth and on the far shelves, brocades, silks and ...

"You made them! You made the monstrosities!" he burst out accusingly.

"I beg your pardon?" said Alison, straightening up.

"You made yon horrible dresses my aunts are wearing. There's the cloth, yon green and puce stuff on the shelf. How could ye?"

Alison, dignified, looked him straight in the eye.

"What is wrong with the gowns, pray?"

"Ye've taken twa foolish, gullible spinster ladies and made them look ridiculous. They shouldnae be wearing yon colours at their age."

"Are ye telling me that ladies of a certain age should gi'e up wearing what pleases them and become invisible? The Misses McFadzean chose those colours and styles. I believe in giving my clients what they want. Your aunts enjoy wearing those dresses. Would ye deny them that pleasure?"

"But they look like the vegetables ye see in the mercats in Paris."

"Oh aye, you've been to Paris and therefore are an arbiter of taste. Let me tell ye, they would hae looked a lot worse if I'd given in tae a' their demands. I managed tae tone them doon quite a bit. Now, I believe these are the laces the Misses McFadzean ordered. Please gi'e them my best regards. I'll bid ye guid day, sir," she finished, still dignified, although her eyes sparkled dangerously and there were two spots of colour in her cheeks.

Tom glared at her for a moment, biting back a furious reply, then snatched up the lace and with a muttered "Guid day", strode out of the shop.

*

As he rode home, he was still seething. To his mind, the girl was exploiting the gullibility of his maiden aunts, no doubt fleecing them without scruple and worse, deliberately mocking them.

The ride home did little to soothe him, so when he barged

into the kitchen he was in a dangerous mood. The sight which greeted him did nothing for his temper. Everyone was bustling about and there was tension in the air. Jeanie was stirring the stock pot and tutting, the maids were chopping mounds of vegetables and Bob, called in once more from the stable, was doing something elaborate with spun sugar.

"What's happening?" demanded Tom.

"Company," said Bob shortly.

"What? When? Who?"

"The nicht, and we didnae ken onything aboot it till twa hours since. It's Mr Cunningham the wine merchant and his fancy French wife and his brither the kirk elder."

"And yer aunts are coming as weel," grumbled Jeannie. "An' forbye, the butler's no' weel again and Bob has tae help serve."

Too late, Tom remembered that he'd been too angry to go back and deliver the lace to his aunts. All his resentment against the grey-eyed dressmaker welled up again, mingled with self-pity at his whole situation. He grabbed a carrot from the table, dodged Jeannie's wooden spoon and went to stew in his room until supper-time.

*

Three hours later he was seated between his aunt Euphemia, dressed in her puce satin with an elaborate feathered turban on her head, and Mrs Cunningham, whose elegant grey silk gown glowing with discreet pearls set off her creamy skin, black hair and alluring dark eyes.

The evening sun shining through the tall windows picked out the snowy damask tablecloth, the delicate china and sparkling crystal glasses as well as the jovial face of Sir Malcolm and the feathers nodding on the Misses McFadzeans' headgear as their eager heads turned this way and that in search of gossip. The long, gloomy features of Mr. James Cunningham, elder of the kirk, contrasted with the pleasant, open face of his brother Richard, wine merchant.

Jeanie and the two kitchen maids deftly removed the soup plates as Bob, trailing a faint scent of stable, replenished the guests' glasses.

Tom sighed, told himself to cheer up and set himself to be pleasant to Mrs Cunningham.

"So how do you find Ayr, Madame?" he enquired.

"I have been here for two years now and it is pleasant enough," she replied, "but I do miss my home town."

"Where are you from, if I may ask?"

"Bordeaux. It is where I met Monsieur Coningamme, when he was there buying wine. We married soon after, and here I am." A shadow of regret passed over her lovely face. "Summer is usually not too bad here," she added, "but I hate the winters. So cold, so wet. I miss the sunshine and of course, Bordeaux is cosmopolitan, Ayr is not."

She gave a pretty shrug and moved closer to Tom.

"And you, Monsieur, I believe you also know France? You were in Paris, *n'est-ce pas?*" There was a mocking glint in her dark eyes which showed she had heard all about Tom's adventures there.

"Yes, I have just returned," replied Tom stiffly, hoping she would change the subject.

"And did you like France?"

"Yes, it's an interesting country."

"And the French?"

"Very hospitable," muttered Tom, feeling he was starting to blush. Finding it difficult to sustain her gaze he dropped his eyes, realising too late that he was now staring at her very attractive *décolleté*.

He was aware that conversation had flagged around the table. Mr James Cunningham, never very loquacious, had a face like a wet Sunday in Tarbolton, the plumes on his aunts' turbans were dancing wildly and at the other end of the table his mother and Mr Richard Cunningham were directing curious stares in their direction.

"And our French women?" continued Mrs Cunningham, blithely unconcerned. "Were they to your liking?"

"*She's only teasing,*" thought Tom. "*Don't pay any mind.*"

Mrs Cunningham obviously expected a reply. She leaned closer, and he caught the elusive scent of her perfume as her left breast almost brushed his sleeve.

"They're very ..." he searched wildly for a suitable adjective "... accommodating."

There was a sharp intake of breath around the table, an audible "Tsk, tsk" from the Misses McFadzean and looking up, Tom saw Bob standing by the sideboard, staring fixedly at the opposite wall, his shoulders shaking with suppressed laughter.

"I'm sure they were, Monsieur Tom, and they would find you delightful company, just as I do," said Mrs Cunningham graciously, turning her attention to the next course which was being served. "Ah, pie."

*

Later, when the candles had been lit and the company was tucking into orange cream with sugar caramel biscuits, Mrs Cunningham turned to Miss Euphemia, saying "I do admire your gown, Miss McFadzean. The colour is somewhat ... unusual, but the cut and finish are excellent. Do you have it from Edinburgh or maybe London?"

Both Misses McFadzean visibly preened.

"Not at all," said Miss Effie, "we have a very skilful seamstress here in Ayr, Miss Alison Fleming. She and her father have a business in the Sandgate."

On hearing the name Mr. James Cunningham, who hitherto had taken little part in the conversation, although he had managed to pack a considerable amount of food into his skeletal frame, burst out, "Yon shameless hussy!"

All eyes turned to him. His mouth, a mere slit in his saturnine face, opened and he went on in his hoarse hectoring voice:

"Gilbert Fleming had nae business makin' her his associate.

Her place is in the hoose, makin' a hame for her faither, no' encouragin' the matrons o' Ayr tae deck themsel's in gaudy colours an' fancy geegaws."

"She is extremely good at what she does," observed Lady Margaret. "Don't the Scriptures tell us to make the maist o' oor talents?"

"Indeed, Madam," said the kirk elder repressively, "but a woman's place is in the hame."

"So you are saying, Monsieur," said Mrs Cunningham, "that women should not be educated?"

"They should learn tae cook and mend and keep hoose. Mair than that is dangerous in a woman."

"How so?" enquired Mrs Cunningham.

"Women should ken their place and be in all things subservient to their maisters, that is, their faithers and husbands."

"Perhaps, sir," said Mrs Cunningham, "that is why you have never married. You have never found such a paragon of womanly virtue."

There was an ominous silence. James Cunningham's jaw moved alarmingly as he tried to suppress an explosion of anger.

"That's as may be, Madam," he said at last, "but we hae seen what happens to women when they hae a wee bit knowledge. They stray from the righteous path and consort wi' the forces o' darkness."

Sir Malcolm interposed calmly, before the women could react. "I think we may say we hae progressed since women were burned as witches, if that is what ye were inferring. I am glad we live in mair enlightened times."

"Ye think so, dae ye?" retorted the elder. "Weel, I've heard it said that young Mistress Fleming's grand-dame was an Osborne. She's likely descended directly frae thon Maggie, that was a famous witch in these parts."

"And what of it?" said Lady Margaret. "Nothing was ever proved against puir Maggie, and my husband is right. We hae gone beyond those times o' superstition and horror."

James Cunningham looked as if he would happily light the faggots under Lady Margaret himself for daring to express an opinion, but remembering that he was a guest at her table, said no more.

Sir Malcolm signalled to Bob to replenish the glasses and the talk turned to other things. Tom, for his part, was intrigued to hear of Alison Fleming's supposed ancestry and resolved to find out more. He reached for his glass and turned again to Mrs Cunningham.

CHAPTER 3

Wednesday August 8th

The next morning Tom had a headache and a marked reluctance to get up and face the world. At breakfast, there was no sign of either parent, much to his relief. David had gone off early to the fields but Kate was there, eager for details of the previous evening.

"Jeanie says ye were very taken wi' Mrs Cunningham," she observed, as she spread honey on a bannock.

"It was an interesting evening," said her brother. "Should ye be eating that much honey? It's no' guid for ye."

"She says Bob says ye couldnae keep yer eyes off her dugs."

Tom groaned and made a hasty retreat. Keeping out of Bob's way, he quickly saddled Sadie and galloped off towards the coast, hoping that the sea air would clear his head and lighten his mood. He rode up to the Heads of Ayr and reined in, catching his breath at the beauty of the scene. It was a lovely morning. A few fluffy white clouds rode high in the bright blue sky as Tom's gaze followed the hazy blue line of the Carrick coast stretching away towards the south while the gulls wheeled and called overhead. Ailsa Craig looked friendly today and he thought for the first time that his home country was maybe not so bad after all.

He rode on south past Dunure and on to Culzean, where the Kennedy family had had their ancient keep transformed into a stately modern dwelling. Tom dismounted near the farm buildings and sat down on a low stone dyke to admire the scene. The original castle, a towering keep on the lonely clifftop, had been incorporated into a modern mansion house with a sweeping driveway and well-kept gardens. The gleaming walls and tall, wide windows spoke of the wealth and prosperity of peaceful times while retaining a ghostly echo of a violent past. The genius of the architect, Robert Adam, was obvious, as was the tireless labour of the countless workmen who had transformed the place.

A line from Voltaire came into Tom's mind "*Il faut cultiver son jardin.*" Architects like Robert Adam certainly made the most of their talents, and Tom reflected ruefully that the same could not be said of himself. His inner garden had grown many weeds over the past months. He needed an aim in life and this building inspired him. A thought struck him. His father knew Robert Adam – maybe he, Tom, could become an architect.

The day was suddenly full of promise and the sun, peeping from behind a cloud, turned the waters of the Firth to shining silver as Tom mounted and galloped off homewards, his head full of castles in Spain.

He was whistling as he took the stairs at Barnessie two at a time and the ancestors' portraits seemed to be, if not exactly smiling, looking at him encouragingly. Arriving outside his father's study he took a deep breath, then knocked. As he entered he noticed that his father, seated behind his large desk, was hastily drawing forward a large legal tome to hide what he had just been reading.

"Come awa' in, Thomas," said Sir Malcolm. "What hae ye been up tae?"

"I've just been oot tae Culzean tae see the new castle. It's a magnificent piece o' work an' I thocht.." he hesitated.

"Aye?"

"I was wondering, could I maybe gang in for architecture? Would Mr Adam or his brither take me on?"

"Dae ye think so?" His father fixed him with a keen stare.

"I thocht if ye asked him maybe ..." Tom's voice trailed off as he noticed his father's expression.

"Are ye serious? Ye've nae training, nae aptitude for it, an' it's the first time ye've expressed an interest. Ye're guid wi' figures, aye, an' ye've a ready tongue, but what aboot imagination? Forbye, ye cannae draw..."

Tom opened his mouth to object, but his father hadn't finished.

"An' if ye think I'll pay for mair education, ye've another think coming. Dinnae look sae dooncast, laddie, ye've had an offer."

"But I've got tae dae something," groaned Tom, then realising what his father had just said, "...an offer?"

"Aye. I dinnae ken why, for ye were staring at his wife's bosom like a famished gaberlunzie, but ye impressed Mr. Cunningham yestreen."

"Did I?" Tom couldn't believe it. He was trying to forget the embarrassment of the previous evening.

"Aye. He tellt me efterwards ye were very courteous and dignified. He kens his wife's an awfu' flirt. Anyway, he's got a vacancy for a clerk in his warehouse and says it's yours if ye want it. He was worried ye'd think it's beneath ye but I tellt him ye'd be pleased tae work for him."

"Wha says so?" Tom was furious. A clerk! It *was* beneath him, especially after his training in Paris. He imagined himself in a dusty warehouse down on the quays, totting up rows of figures day in, day out, till he was stooped and old and grey.

"I say so," said his father sternly. "Face it, laddie. Ye've nae money, ye'll get nae mair frae me, an' ye've gye few prospects. The world disnae owe ye a living, an' nor dae I. Ye have tae mak' yer ain way noo. I've accepted Mr Cunningham's offer on your behalf. Ye start the morn's morn."

Sir Malcolm watched impassively as his son flung out of the room, just managing not to slam the door, then sighed and drawing the latest Scots Magazine out from under the law books, went on reading about Lord Monboddo and the orang-utan.

CHAPTER 4

Thursday August 9th

———

The next morning at eight, Tom was tethering Sadie in the stable yard behind Richard Cunningham's warehouse on the North Quay. The morning had dawned bright and fair, which did nothing to lighten his feeling of gloom. Too late, he realised that the last few days had been a holiday; now he was going to have to buckle down. He sighed, straightened his shoulders and began climbing the rickety wooden stairs to the offices. At the top, he pushed open the door and blinked as his eyes adjusted to the relative gloom inside.

"There ye are, lad," said a kind voice. "Come awa' in." Richard Cunningham came forward to shake hands with his new employee.

The room they were standing in looked over the yard, with the stables opposite and on either side, the large double doors to the warehouses. Beneath the offices was a wide arched entrance, through which men were carrying casks and rolling barrels which they had just unloaded from a tall ship berthed at the quay. The noise of rumbling barrels echoed through the building, drowning the squawking of the seagulls overhead.

The office was furnished with two tall desks, one with a high stool, and shelves laden with ledgers. Two small windows, one on either side of the door, looked out over the yard; a door on the opposite wall led to Mr Cunningham's own office, into which Tom was now invited. It was a larger room, with a handsome mahogany desk on a Turkish carpet, two deep tapestry-upholstered chairs and prints of local scenes on the walls – Ailsa Craig, Dunure Castle and the ruins of Crossraguel Abbey. The room was light and airy, in contrast to the cramped outer office. The tall windows afforded a view of the bustling quays on either side of the river and, on the opposite bank, the huddled ruins of Cromwell's fort commanding the mouth of the estuary.

"I'm glad you're gonnae work wi' us, Tom," said Mr Cunningham. "We'll start by showing ye the business and get ye tae help keep the books. But your faither says ye ken a lot aboot wine, so maybe there'll be mair interesting things for ye tae dae once ye've learned a bit."

This prospect lightened Tom's mood somewhat but just then he heard a step on the outside stair and turned to see a skinny, carroty-haired youth of about his own age framed in the doorway.

"Come awa' in, Mungo," said Richard Cunningham, "and meet your new colleague. This is Tom Boyd, and he'll be working wi' ye. Tom, this is Mungo McGillivray, my other clerk. He'll show ye the ropes."

Mungo fixed Tom with a belligerent blue stare and muttered something about not needing any help. "I can manage the books fine masel'."

"Aye, but I'm looking tae expand the business, and Tom here's had experience frae Paris. He kens aboot wine, and he'll be a lot o' help there," said Mr Cunningham, with an encouraging smile for Tom. "For noo, I want ye tae show him the books and go over the accounts wi' him. After that, ye can tak him ower tae the warehoose. Dinna fash yersel', laddie, there's mair than enough work for twa."

For answer, Mungo merely grunted. Finally, "Come on, then," he said, flouncing with ill grace into the outer office. "That's your desk," he said, indicating the shabbier of the two, the one without a stool. For the next hour, he proceeded to pull down ledger after ledger and run through the columns of figures at full speed, so that Tom had no chance of understanding anything beyond the names of a few suppliers in France, some of whom were known to him, and some customers in Scotland. He had no idea at this speed how the book-keeping system worked, or how far back the accounts reached, as many of them seemed to bear no dates. He told himself not to worry; he could go over the books at his leisure once Mungo found something else to do.

Sure enough, "Got it, Monsewer?" asked Mungo eventually.

Tom did not rise to the bait, saying merely, "I'll just gang ower the last bit again masel'", whereupon Mungo took himself off to his own desk, settled himself on his high stool and watched with open scorn as Tom carefully went through the figures, trying to ignore his colleague's distracting tactics – drumming his fingers on the desk, muttering to himself and indulging in a prolonged sneezing fit. Tom would have said something had he not been conscious of his father's dire warnings about last chances and his own determination to cultivate his garden. Besides, he liked Mr Cunningham and in spite of Mungo's efforts, he was beginning to make sense of the accounts.

Eventually Mungo sighed deeply and pushed himself off his stool.

"I'll show ye the warehoose noo."

Tom followed him down the creaking wooden stairs and across the yard, passing a group of men heaving casks onto carts bound for Glasgow, Edinburgh and Dumfries. "Oot the way, laddie," sneered one of them, elbowing Tom in the ribs as he came a little too close. Tom wanted to remonstrate, but Mungo had already disappeared through the big double doors on the right, and he hurried to follow.

Entering the warehouse, his senses were assailed by the sour-sweet, woody smell of wine and the heady aroma of spirits from the casks and bottles on the heavy stands which stretched away into the gloom. A stocky, powerful figure with close-cropped brown hair and a livid scar on his broad face stood near the doorway with a sheaf of papers in his hand, ticking off the casks and bottles as they were carried to the carts.

"Adam," said Mungo, "This here's..."

"Haud yer wheesht, ye wee gommerel," snarled the man. "Bide there till I've feenished." He went back to his lists while Tom looked round curiously and Mungo twitched impatiently.

Finally the man Adam folded his papers and turned his attention to them. "Wha's this?" he asked, staring inquisitively at Tom.

"Tom Boyd, the new clerk," said Mungo. "I've tae show him the warehoose."

"I'll dae that, you get back tae the office." As Mungo slouched off, he continued. "Adam Kennedy, at your service. I'm the head warehooseman. Ye'll be Sir Malcolm's boy? The one that's been tae France?" His tone throughout bordered on insolence and ended with a leer. "I heard Mr Cunningham had ta'en ye on, but I cannae think why." He shook his head sorrowfully. "Anyway, I'll show ye the warehooses."

For the next fifteen minutes, Tom was taken on a lightning tour of the two warehouses, following Adam Kennedy as he strode around with a rolling, confident gait, pointing out the stores of wine, spirits, tea, coffee and salt.

"This must be worth a pickle," said Tom. "Are ye no' scared o' thieves?"

"Scared?" Kennedy spat contemptuously. "Nae fear. It's a' weel locked up at nicht." And he stared at Tom, as if accusing him of having designs on the stock. "So, hae ye seen enough? Get awa' back tae yer office, then. Me an' the lads tak' care o' everything doon here." He glanced meaningfully at the two hefty young men lounging by the door, one of whom Tom recognised as the man who had elbowed him earlier. "Back tae work wi' ye, Geordie, Wullie," ordered Kennedy.

Back in the office Tom found Mungo, looking industrious for once, writing out invoices in a fine copperplate hand. "Ye can dae the envelopes," he said graciously. "There's a list on yer desk."

The rest of the day passed in not very companionable

silence. Mungo gave Tom a few easy tasks to do and let him spend some time going through the ledgers. His manner seemed to have moved from open scorn, through resentment to something like indifference, for which Tom was grateful. Nevertheless, at the end of the day he was glad to saddle up Sadie and set out for home.

*

At supper-time in the cosy family dining-room off the formal one, Tom looked round the table and felt glad to be back with his family after the trials of the day.

"Let's see what Bo ... Jeanie has got for us," said his mother, removing the lid of the dish to release the fragrant aroma of a tempting rabbit stew. There was a pause as she dished it out and handed round the vegetables. Tom could see that Kate was squirming with impatience and his father and brother were trying only slightly more successfully to contain their curiosity. He braced himself for the inevitable questions.

"Weel, son," said Lady Margaret once everyone had been served.

"It was fine," he said, fearing his father's anger if he dared complain. "Mr Cunningham was very ..."

"Accommodating?" piped up Kate, who had heard from Jeanie about Tom's most recent use of that adjective. Her mother silenced her with a look.

"... pleasant," said Tom. "The business seems tae be thriving. I saw the books and warehooses, and helped wi' some invoices."

Kate yawned theatrically, earning another warning look from her mother.

"Mr Cunningham said I might be involved in expanding the business," continued Tom with a repressive stare at his sister.

"Hoo mony does he employ?" asked Sir Malcolm.

"Weel, there's twa lads work in the warehooses, and twa or three mair come by tae help wi' loadin' and unloadin'. There's a ship in frae France the day. And the heid warehooseman, Adam

Kennedy." Tom shivered, remembering the reception he'd had from that quarter.

"Adam Kennedy?" asked David. "I ken o' him. Ye'll no' want tae cross him, he's a hard man. I'm surprised Mr Cunningham employs him. Ye saw his scar?" Tom nodded. "They say he got that in a fight wi' an excise man."

"Ye think he's been mixed up in smuggling?" Lady Margaret was shocked.

"It's what they hint at," said David, "but wha kens? Maybe it was the excise man the thief. Naebody kens the truth o' it. Onyway, Tom, ye'd best keep oot o' his way."

"Are there just you and Mr Cunningham in the office?" asked his mother.

"Weel, Mr Cunningham's only there sometimes. There's his other clerk, the one that showed me the books an' got me started. Mungo McGillivray, he's cried."

"Mungo," said David. "I ken him weel. He was at skule wi' me. What dae ye think tae him?"

"He was civil enough."

"But no' very ... accommodating," teased his brother. "Aye, that would be Mungo. Red hair, plooks an' a chip on his shooder. Ye'll need tae watch oot for him, an a'. He lives wi' his mither in a wee hoose in Mill Street, doon by the tannery. She's a puir soul, no' richt in the heid, aye beggin' scraps in the mercats."

Tom suddenly felt more kindly disposed towards Mungo. No wonder he was so resentful; he probably thought he was going to lose his place to Tom.

"Just see ye stick in at the job, Thomas," said his father, wiping up the last of his plate of stew. "I see there's a rhubarb pie. I hope it's yin o' Bob's."

CHAPTER 5

Friday August 10th

Next day, after a morning spent writing out invoices to the accompaniment of a deafening silence from Mungo, Tom was given an hour's break and decided to cross to the South Quay and take a walk along the shore past Cromwell's fort. The day was overcast and dull, with rain spitting in the wind.

He passed the fort at the mouth of the river, built by Cromwell over a hundred years previously to keep the citizens of Ayr in line; now abandoned, it was already falling into ruin. There was less of it than Tom remembered from his childhood; the townspeople were gradually removing the stones for domestic building.

The stiff breeze pulled at Tom's coat as he started off along the shore. It was noisy, heavy going on the shingle and after a while he stopped to pick up a flat stone and, taking careful aim, he threw it hard and flat into the water. It bounced four times before sinking; Tom was satisfied he had not lost his touch.

"Is that the best ye can dae?" called a voice. Turning, he saw Alison Fleming standing further up on the sandy part of the shore. The wind tugged at her blue woollen plaid and her hair, strands of which were escaping her plain linen cap and blowing around her face, and put colour in her pale cheeks. She scrambled down the beach to join him at the water's edge.

"I'm a bit oot o' practice," admitted Tom. "I havenae skited chucky stanes for years."

"I dinnae suppose it's a Parisian pastime," laughed Alison. She selected a flat blue-grey stone and expertly sent it skimming into the waves. "Five!" she cried. "Your turn."

Tom needed no further invitation and soon they were skimming stones like the children they had been not that long before, leaping and stumbling on the shingle and calling challenges, their laughter borne away on the wind.

Finally they stopped for breath and looked at each other, in accord for the first time.

"What brings ye tae the shore?" asked Alison. Tom explained about his job at Cunningham's.

"I come doon here whiles masel'," said Alison. "It clears the heid when I'm stuck wi' the figures or I cannae think how best tae cut some cloth. I've a new order for some stays for Mrs Cunningham – that'll be your new employer's wife – an' I want tae dae a guid job."

"Has she been tae see ye already?" asked Tom, surprised. He explained about the supper party and the Misses McFadzeans' recommendation.

"Weel, I've them tae thank for it," replied Alison. "She's an important client and I just hope I can gi'e satisfaction. She usually has *modistes* from Edinburgh and London."

"It's guid she's gi'en ye an order in spite o' what her brither-in-law says," said Tom, then realised too late that Alison would be curious to know more and would not like what she heard. Sure enough,

"What dae ye mean?" she demanded.

"It was Mr James Cunningham, the elder. He said women should keep hoose and ken their place."

"Did he noo? And did he say that generally, or did he talk aboot me?"

"I think ye did mention you . . ." Tom hesitated as he realised his evasive tone was cutting no ice with Alison.

"What exactly did he say?"

Tom swallowed hard, then plunged into as exact a summary of the conversation as he could manage, careful to omit the "shameless hussy" reference and include his mother's and Mrs Cunningham's attempts to defend her. Unfortunately, he forgot to stop when he reached the part about Maggie Osborne, the witch.

"So that's it," said Alison furiously. "Yon man, for a' he's a kirk elder, is a holier-than-thou slanderer. Aye, Maggie Osborne was my ancestor, but she was nae witch, just a clever woman brought doon by jealous, mealy-mouthed matrons and kirk elders and hounded tae death just because she was different." She paused for breath, her eyes sparkling dangerously. "An' you, Tom Boyd, I thocht ye'd ken better than tae gi'e ony credence tae thon lies, still less fling them in my face. Guid-day tae ye." And she turned and stumbled clumsily away from him up the shingle, her eyes blinded by angry tears.

Tom wanted to go after her, to explain that he was on her side and hadn't meant to offend her, but he had a feeling she wouldn't listen. As he turned back towards the town, he caught sight of a tall, still figure standing some way off; James Cunningham, watching him like a black corbie eying a juicy corpse.

*

Alison hurried along the Sandgate, still fuming at Tom Boyd. Why did he annoy her so much? One minute, they had been laughing together like carefree children, the next he was repeating, with relish it seemed, things he must have known she had no wish to hear. The fact that she had asked him to do so did not cross her mind. "Graceless gowk!" she muttered. "If that's what Paris does tae ye, I'm never gaun there."

She was so angry she didn't notice the bundle of rags in the doorway of her shop and stumbled over it. To her surprise, the bundle squawked indignantly and made to struggle to its feet, cursing the while. Alison saw a small hunched woman with dull, greasy red hair and a wild, haggard face, reeking strongly of ale.

"I beg your pardon, mistress," she said. "I didnae see ye there."

"Aye," said the woman bitterly. "Your sort never dae."

On closer inspection, the woman looked much younger than Alison had first thought, but she was obviously in difficulty, though whether from drink or injury it was impossible to say,

"Whaur dae ye bide, mistress?" she asked. "Can I see ye hame?"

The woman muttered another curse, staggered a few steps and collapsed against the wall.

"Come awa' wi' ye, mistress," said Alison. "Tak' my airm," then staggered herself as the woman clutched her arm in a surprisingly strong grip and leaned heavily on her.

"Mill Street," she croaked.

"*Well,*" thought Alison, "*at least she has a hame.*"

Mill Street ran behind the High Street, down by the river, and contained a brewery, a tannery and the hovels of the poor.

They set off, staggering back down the Sandgate under the curious stares of the good townspeople of Ayr, turned right under the grim walls of the Tolbooth and passed through the vennel to the High Street, where a few local lads began to follow them, jeering.

"Haw there, Paisley Annie, wha's yer friend?"

"She looks a likely lass. Hoo much is she askin'?"

The woman let go of Alison's arm to aim a kick at the nearest boy, missed and fell backwards into the midden. Alison made haste to help her up from the rotting heap and they carried on to Mill Street, where the combined stink of fermenting barley, animal hides and urine almost made Alison retch. She struggled on, however, and presently the woman Annie turned in at the meanest hovel and staggered towards a low stool, one of the few items of furniture in the dark, dirty room.

Alison followed, catching her breath at the squalor of her surroundings. Spying a pail in the corner, she dipped the end of her plaid in the brackish water and tried to wash the worst of the muck from Annie's hands and face. All the strength had gone out of the woman and she submitted meekly to Alison's ministrations.

"Let be," she said finally. "I'll be fine noo I'm hame."

Alison stood back and looked round the room. There was no fire in the mean hearth and the air was damp and clammy. Apart from the stool where Annie sat slumped there was a rough wooden recess bed with a straw mattress, a rickety wooden table and an ancient press. An old iron cooking pot lay abandoned on the hearth and empty bottles littered the floor.

"Would ye no' like tae lie doon?" asked Alison, indicating the bed, for she could see that Annie was near collapse.

"It's no' my bed, it's Mungo's."

"Mungo?"

"My son," said Annie with unexpected dignity. "He's a guid laddie."

"So whaur dae ye sleep?"

Annie pointed vaguely at a pile of dirty straw in the far corner. Alison could not believe that a mother could speak with pride of a son who kept the only bed to himself and let his mother sleep on stinking straw on the floor.

"Whaur is Mungo noo?" she demanded sharply.

"At his work. He'll be hame soon. Ye'd better go. He'd no' want tae find ye here. He disnae haud wi' company."

Alison wanted to wait until the son came home and give him a piece of her mind, but seeing her hesitate, Annie struggled to her feet and shouted "Get oot o' ma hoose. Ye're no' wanted here."

Behind the anger, Alison could sense fear so, not wanting to cause trouble, she made for the door. As she pulled it to behind her she thought she heard Annie whisper "God bless ye, dearie."

As she hurried back to the shop, Annie decided she must do what she could for the woman called Paisley Annie and resolved to find out more about her and her son.

*

Tom strode into the warehouse yard, his thoughts in a turmoil. He was cursing himself for mentioning Maggie Osborne to Alison and trying to understand the unease he had felt at the sight of James Cunningham. As he started up the stairs to the offices he heard a clatter of hooves behind him and turned to see Mrs Cunningham, clad in a russet velvet riding habit, reining in a magnificent chestnut mare. All the men in the yard stopped to admire the sight, but as Adam Kennedy moved to help her dismount she shot him a scornful look and called, "Monsieur Tom, aidez-moi à descendre, s'il vous plaît."

Tom, blushing, stepped forward and held out his arms. A moment later he was standing with his hands on the shoulders of her expensive russet velvet, conscious of her warm breath and elusive French perfume. They stood for a moment, very close, then she turned to Kennedy. "See to my horse, Monsieur Kennedy. Is my husband in the office?"

"Yes ma'am," muttered Kennedy, touching his bonnet but shooting a murderous look at Tom.

"Then come, Monsieur Tom." Laying a surprisingly strong hand on his arm, she gathered up her skirts and crossed the courtyard, seemingly oblivious to the hot stares of the men. As they mounted the steps Tom could feel waves of envy and resentment from below and was aware of the cool mockery of the woman at his side.

Mungo started guiltily as they entered the front office, quickly concealing some papers under the open ledger on his desk. Tom pretended not to have noticed. He didn't trust Mungo yet.

Mrs Cunningham paused at her husband's door. "Merci de m'avoir accompagnée, Monsieur Tom," she breathed with a dazzling smile.

Tom, trying hard not to blush, gave his best bow as she disappeared into the inner office.

"Quite the braw gentleman, aren't we?" sneered Mungo. "Gallivantin' roon' the toon an' makin' sheep's eyes at the boss's wife while ithers dae a' the wark."

Tom instantly felt ashamed.

"Sorry," he muttered. "Look, Mungo, I ken it maybe looks

like I'm after your job, but Mr Cunningham aye says there's work enough for baith o' us. Forbye, I ken ye work hard and I'm willing tae be guided by you. I dinnae want ony bad feeling between us."

Mungo stared at him and let an uncomfortable silence stretch between them. Finally, though, he grinned and said, "A' richt, we'll try tae get on. Just as long as ye remember I'm the boss."

They worked on at their books through the afternoon. Mungo now and then darted glances at the closed inner door, through which could be heard a low murmur of voices, rolling his eyes and conveying to Tom through a series of unmistakeable gestures just what he thought was going on inside. Mungo was a talented mimic, so that when the door finally opened and Mr and Mrs Cunningham passed them on the way to the stairs Tom had to try hard not to burst out laughing. Once they were gone,

"Ye dinnae think . . .?" asked Tom.

"Oh aye, they get up tae all sorts. She's a wanton hussy, thon yin. Ye'll need tae watch yersel', I saw the way she looked at ye."

Tom sighed and went back to his invoices.

*

The weather had brightened during the afternoon and Tom felt his spirits lift as he drew near home. As he made his way through the yard after stabling Sadie he heard the familiar creak of the old swing which hung from the apple tree in the walled kitchen garden, and he found Kate swinging thoughtfully back and forth, munching an apple.

"Ye'll mak yersel' sick, wee sister," he admonished. "Thae apples arenae ripe yet."

"Ye're right for once, big brither." Kate made a face and threw the apple away. "Hoo's the job?"

Tom settled on the bench by the wall beside her. "No' bad. I think I'm gettin' the hang o' it, but . . ."

"But what?"

"Mr Cunningham's fine, but the ithers are still no' that friendly. I'm getting' on better wi' Mungo, but ..." Into his mind came a picture of Mungo hiding papers and this prompted another thought.

"But ..." repeated Kate.

Tom hesitated, finally saying, "I've a feeling mair goes on than meets the eye. They're no' keen on me gaun intae the warehoose, an' Mungo was hidin' somethin' the day."

Kate's eyes widened.

"Smuggling!" she said. "Even I ken there's a lot o' that goes on."

"Maybe, but Cunningham's is a respectable business. Forbye, it's thriving. I dinnae think they'd need to turn tae smuggling."

"Mr Cunningham maybe disnae ken what they're up tae in the warehoose. Or maybe he just disnae want tae ken."

Tom thought, not for the first time, that his wee sister was too clever by half. She had put into words what until then had only been vague, half-formed suspicions in his mind.

"Mrs Cunningham came by the day," he said, in an attempt to change the subject. Kate was instantly diverted.

"Oh, she's so elegant, so French. I want tae gang tae France some day." She sighed.

"Maybe ye will."

"Dae ye still miss Paris?"

"Aye, but ..." Tom surprised himself with his answer, "no' as much as I did."

"I'm glad. It's guid tae hae ye hame, Tom."

"It's guid tae be hame," said Tom, meaning it. "Come on, wee sister, it's supper time. Best no' tae mention smuggling, eh? Let's keep it between oorsels, for noo." He put a brotherly arm round her shoulder and they set off towards the house.

CHAPTER 6

Monday August 13th

The day was overcast again and the first drops of rain were falling as Alison called goodbye to her father and set off along the Sandgate with a basket over her arm and a determined step. This was to give her courage, for she was going back to Paisley Annie's.

"*You're a fool,*" said one part of herself. "*She'll no' want charity, she might be roarin' fu' already, and what if Mungo's there?*"

"*We'll just have tae see,*" said her other half. "*Ye can't not go.*"

Mill Street was already a hive of activity as she approached Annie's hovel. The stink from the tannery and brewery was as overpowering as she remembered, and filthy prentice boys crossed and recrossed the narrow street carrying soaking animal hides and pails of fermenting hops.

"Watch yersel', Miss," cried a lad as he barged past Alison, spilling foul-smelling liquid from his bucket on to her shoes.

Alison jumped the gutter which ran up the middle of the street and knocked tentatively on Annie's door. There was no answer, and no sound from within. Cautiously she pressed the latch and opened the door. The smell of drink and human waste hit her and as her eyes grew accustomed to the darkness she made out the figure huddled on the dirty straw, nursing an empty bottle and crooning to herself.

Alison put her basket on the dirty table and went to kneel by Annie.

"Annie, it's me, Alison. Ye remember?"

Annie looked round wildly, belched loudly and clutched the ragged ends of her kirtle together over her greasy shift. Gradually her eyes focused on Alison and as recognition dawned she favoured her with a gummy smile.

"Aw, it's the bonnie wee lass," she said fondly. "Ye were here afore."

"Aye, I've brocht ye some things."

"Tae drink?" asked Annie hopefully.

"Tae eat. Just some bannocks and cheese, a wee bit butter and a couple o' eggs."

A strange proud light came into Annie's eyes. She attempted to straighten up, glared at Alison and sneered, "Charity. I don't need your charity." She spat in the straw.

"Not charity," said Alison, "just a wee gift from a friend. And ye'll get nae mair if that's how ye feel." For a few moments the two women glared at each other, then Annie sighed.

"Eggs, did ye say? I used tae like a nice boiled egg."

"Can I make a fire?" asked Alison, indicating the cold hearth

"Nae wood."

"Well it's a guid thing I brocht a few sticks."

Alison set to work. She swept the hearth for the first time in ages, judging by the coughing fit the work provoked, set and lit a meagre fire, then fetched some stray lumps of coal from among the stones by the tannery gate. She soon had a decent fire going and set water from the butt in the back yard to boil. While waiting, she swept the packed earth floor as best she could and pulled aside the grimy piece of sacking which covered the small back window. She could see down to the river, where a lone swan glided gracefully as the ever-present gulls wheeled overhead.

Ten minutes later she set a fairly clean plate of oat bannocks, cheese and a boiled egg in its shell on the table and turned back to Annie. She helped her over to the chair. Annie eyed the egg greedily, seized the spoon Alison had found in the table drawer, broke the shell and began to eat, slowly at first, then more hungrily. Finally, she wiped up the yolk with the last mouthful of bannock and sat back with a sigh.

"Guid," she pronounced.

Tentatively, Alison said, "Could ye no' dae that for yersel', whiles?"

Annie's face clouded over.

"Ower much bother. It's easier just tae drink"

"Why dae ye need tae drink?"

Annie lowered her voice.

"Maybe ... tae forget." Then, her voice cracking, a faraway look in her eyes, she began to croon words Alison could scarcely hear.

"How often didst thou pledge and vow
Thou wouldst for aye be mine?"

Then, just as quickly, her expression changed and it was clear she would answer no more questions that day. Alison fetched her basket.

"There's a wee bit mair coal tae keep the fire goin'. I'll come back and see ye the morn."

There was no reply. Annie's mind was obviously far away.

As she made her way home, Alison wondered if she had done any good. One boiled egg wasn't going to wean a woman haunted by her past off the bottle, but at least Annie was warm and fed for an hour or two. Alison was determined to confront the mysterious Mungo and decided to time her next visit differently in the hope of finding him at home.

*

The mysterious Mungo was at his desk, moodily counting up columns of figures. At the other desk, Tom was similarly engaged, but distracted by thoughts of what his sister had said about smuggling. How would they do it? Who would be involved? The most likely were the warehousemen; they were always reluctant to let him in there, as if clerks were not to be involved in the real business of the firm. The excise men could come and inspect at any time without warning, so how did they hide the contraband goods? Did the smuggled goods come in on the regular ships or did they have another source? How were the goods distributed afterwards? Most importantly, was Mr. Cunningham himself involved, the instigator even? He had always struck Tom as an honest man, well respected in Ayr and in Bordeaux, talked of as a future provost. Surely he would not jeopardise his position?

Tom glanced over at Mungo. Was he involved? Tom was aware he hardly knew his fellow clerk, and decided he would start by getting to know him better.

As if on cue, Mungo sighed deeply, threw down his pen and banged the ledger shut.

"It's noon and I'm famished," he declared. "Fancy a bite and a drink?"

"Is it all right if we baith gang oot?"

"Nae bother. We can just lock up for an hour. Mr Cunningham'll no' be in till later." As they went out through the wide doors to the quay, Tom glanced over at the warehouse. As usual, Adam Kennedy was lounging in the doorway like Cerberus guarding the underworld. Tom wondered if he even let Mr Cunningham inside.

A damp drizzle was falling as they crossed the bridge and took the steep vennel down to the High Street, where the fishwives were calling their wares by the cross. The smell of fish mingled with damp dirty wool and excrement caught at Tom's throat. Halfway down, a ragged figure appeared from a doorway and clutched at Mungo's arm.

"Haw there, son, hae ye got a penny for me?"

"No' the noo, mither," muttered Mungo, brushing off her hand. He grasped Tom's arm and hurried him away. They went into the crowded tavern at the corner where Mungo ordered up two measures of ale and some bannocks and cheese, waving aside Tom's offer to pay.

"My shout the day, yours next time."

They shook the rain from their plaids and found two vacant stools near the fire. Mungo launched immediately into a tale about a couple that had had to stand out in the kirk for fornication. Tom waited until he had finished, then said,

"Wha was it?"

"What dae ye mean?"

"Yon woman in the street. She ca'd ye son. Is that yer mither?"

Mungo blushed a fiery red, took a gulp of ale, then muttered, "Aye, that's her."

Tom said nothing.

"Ye're wonderin' why she's in sic a state. It's no' my fault."

"I've heard she begs in the mercats," said Tom. "That's no' safe for her, if she hasnae got a badge."

This obviously touched a raw nerve with Mungo. He leaped to his feet and for a moment Tom thought he would strike him.

"Mind yer ain business, can't ye? Dae I meddle in your affairs? Hae I ever speired what ye were up tae in Paris? Fornication, I've nae doot."

As suddenly as it had come, his anger subsided. He slumped onto his stool and sighed. "Look, my mither's a drunk. She cannae get a beggar's badge for I'm in work. I gi'e her money, but she spends it on drink. Oor hoose is a hovel, an' it's her job tae look efter it, but she disnae ken whaur she is, maist o' the time. I dinnae ken what tae dae. She's gettin' worse an' I cannae thole bein' at hame. I only gang there tae sleep. Just be thankfu' your mither's a saint, no' Paisley Annie."

His voice broke on the last words and he looked on the verge of tears. Tom felt sorry, but all he could think of to say was "Why dae they cry her Paisley Annie?"

"She's frae Paisley, that's why," said Mungo in the weary tones of an adult addressing a small, ignorant child. "She cam' here when she was a lass, she had nae folks, an' she was in service wi' some rich family. She never let on wha they were."

"Why did she leave?"

"She's never said, but it doesnae tak' a brain tae work it oot. She got me an' they turned her awa.'"

"So wha's yer faither?"

"I dinnae ken, an' my mither's never said. I'm a bastard, richt enough," said Mungo with a rueful grimace. "But hey," he went on, "I've got my wits an' a job. At least, for noo," he added with a sly glance at Tom.

"Can ye get it intae yer heid, I'm no' after yer job. Mr Cunningham values you, he said so, and . . ." Tom hesitated, "I'd like tae think we're friends."

"Friends!" crowed Mungo. "Weel, aye, maybe . . ."

Tom clasped him on the shoulder. "Guid man. Weel, we've time for anither afore we need tae get back. My shout this time.

CHAPTER 7

Sunday August 19th

Sunday, and for once the rain stopped and the sun shone on the righteous as they made their way to the kirk. Sir Malcolm decreed that the Boyd family would walk into Ayr for the morning service at the parish church, while Bob followed with the carriage in case the weather changed.

Dressed in their Sunday best, they made their way down the lanes between hawthorn hedges, enjoying the sun on their backs and doing their best to avoid puddles. Sir Malcolm, dressed soberly in his good black coat and tawny brocade waistcoat, gave his arm to Lady Margaret, in quiet dove-grey silk. Behind them came David in his good buff coat, Kate showing off her new black velvet jacket and striped satin kirtle, and Tom in his blue Paris coat.

"Bessie Gibney has tae stand in the kirk the day," said David. "She's had anither wean, an' her no' merrit. It's a relapse this time, so she'll be in front o' the congregation a few times."

"What's a relapse?" inquired Kate.

"It's when a lassie has stood before an' hasnae learned the error o' her ways," said her brother. "Doesnae seem right tae me, the kirk session didnae gang efter the faither."

"Wha's the faither?" asked Tom.

"The De'il only kens. The lassie'll no' say. Like as no' there's a few candidates," he added with a bitter laugh.

By now they were in the streets of Ayr and joining the throng of parishioners making their way towards St John's Parish Church. Everyone was in Sunday best, but not every "best" was equally good. Fine ladies and gentlemen mixed with good burghers in plain broadcloth and poorer folk in flannel and hodden grey. The children of the poor, used to going barefoot, carried their one pair of shoes which they would put on at the church gate and try not to squirm with the unaccustomed pinching during the service.

Once inside the kirk the Boyds nodded and exchanged greetings with friends and acquaintances as they made their way to the family pew where the Misses McFadzean, resplendent in colourful silk and waving plumes, were already installed. Looking round, Tom saw Alison Fleming and a short, stooped gentleman he assumed was her father in a pew not far from theirs. Near the front, the forbidding figure of James Cunningham sat with the other elders of the kirk session, casting censorious eyes over the congregation, his gaze lingering disapprovingly on the bright McFadzean silks. On the far side of the kirk sat his brother Richard and his wife, whose fixed smile concealed, Tom guessed, unfathomable levels of boredom.

The service began, and after the first psalm, sung raggedly to a wheezing organ accompaniment, and the Old Testament reading, delivered in a fire-and-brimstone voice by Mr. James Cunningham, an expectant hush fell on the congregation. A buxom figure, dressed in an old black kirtle with a rough sackcloth cap on her head, emerged from the side and went to stand, trembling slightly, on a stool by the pulpit. Her face, though pale and downcast, was determined, and her lips set firm with the effort not to break down.

"Bessie Gibney," intoned the minister, "you have been found guilty of relapse and have strayed far from the path of righteousness. The sentence of the Kirk Session is that you stand witness before the congregation of this church on four consecutive Sundays, until you come to proper acknowledgement of your repeated ...", here the minister paused and wagged his finger at the unfortunate girl, glowering all the while, "... repeated transgressions of God's holy law. We the congregation will pray that you be brought to true repentance and forsake your wicked ways, so that you may be received again into the fellowship of the righteous."

He continued in this vein for several minutes more during which Tom, who always felt uncomfortable at such moments, risked looking round to see the effect of the minister's words on the congregation. Many were enjoying Bessie's discomfiture, indeed several matrons were tutting audibly. Some were fidgeting uncomfortably while others stared impassively ahead, not risking betraying their opinion. Tom noticed that Alison Fleming was staring at the minister, an expression of undisguised disgust on her face, and James Cunningham was watching Bessie, his eyes glittering. "He's enjoying this," thought Tom, looking on in astonishment as the elder slowly licked his lips.

"Let us pray," said the minister.

*

After the service the congregation slowly dispersed, some remaining in the churchyard to exchange gossip and family views. Seeing his mother in conversation with Alison, Tom approached in time to hear Lady Margaret say, "Tuesday, then, aboot four?"

"That would be fine," replied Alison.

"Good. Ah, Tom. Your aunt has just introduced me to Mistress Fleming. I've a mind tae order a new gown for the autumn ball in the Assembly Rooms."

Tom groaned inwardly. *Not another monstrosity in the family*, he thought. "Er, what kind o' gown?" he enquired. "One like Aunt Letty's?"

Seeing the colour mount in Alison's cheeks, his mother said hastily, "Thomas, ye ken I will choose something fitting, and Mistress Fleming is an expert seamstress. She'll come and measure me this week."

"So ye dinnae need tae worry," added Alison with a pert smile.

Tom felt the need for combat.

"No' as worried as you looked in the kirk the noo," he said. "Or angry, mair like."

"Angry? Of course I was angry. Wha wouldna be? Yon puir lassie havin' tae stand and listen tae the minister haranguing her for her sins? What sins? Whaur was the bairn's faither? Some cowardly coof, taking advantage o' a puir ignorant lassie, then hiding while she's made a spectacle and a laughing-stock for the righteous burghers of Ayr. Hypocrites, all o' them," she added, glaring at Tom. Obviously she numbered him among the hypocrites.

"I'll admit it made me uncomfortable," he said. "I'd forgotten sic things still happened here. But at least they dinnae burn witches ony mair, ye'll be glad tae ken."

Alison reddened and glared at him, remembering their previous conversation on that subject.

"Thomas, that remark was uncalled for," said his mother. "Please excuse my son, Mistress Fleming. He still has some growing up to do."

"No apology necessary," said Alison stiffly. "Here's my faither. I'll bid ye guid-day, ma'am, ... Master Thomas," she added coldly as she turned away.

Lady Margaret took Tom's arm and walked with him towards the kirk yett.

"Was that necessary, Tom?" she asked. "Such a lovely, spirited lass. Why does she seem tae bring oot the worst in you?"

"I dinnae ken, mither. Maybe I don't like that she aye seems tae be right."

"Well, just admit it and be grateful that she is. Noo, let's awa' hame afore the rain starts. Yon clouds look ominous."

CHAPTER 8

Monday August 20th

The next morning, the excise men arrived. Riding into the courtyard at Cunningham's, Tom saw a knot of men huddled round two stern, soberly-clad strangers. He stabled Sadie and hurried to join them.

"We'll look through the accounts first," said the taller of the two, who had introduced himself as Gavin McKie, "then inspect the warehoose."

Tom studied the faces of his fellow workers. Mr Cunningham looked concerned, while Adam Kennedy and the warehousemen looked more open and honest than Tom had ever seen them before. Mungo was watching proceedings with undisguised glee.

"This way, then, gentlemen," said Mr Cunningham, heading towards the stairs to the offices. As he turned to follow him, Tom thought he caught a glimpse of a signal between Kennedy and Geordie McSkimming.

In the office, the excise men began methodically checking the accounts of the imported goods against the sales invoices and stock records.

"Ye've a new clerk, I see," remarked Gavin McKie to Mr Cunningham.

"Aye. This is Tom Boyd, no' lang back frae France. He's made himsel' very useful in the short time he's been wi' us."

"I'm sure he has," said the second excise man, staring hard at Tom. "What were ye daein' in France? I thocht we were at war wi' the Frenchies."

"Er, I worked for a wine merchant. Commerce aye carries on."

"Indeed," said McKie. "Nae doot ye hae some usefu' contacts."

Tom had the uneasy feeling that he was under suspicion. Did they mean contacts among smugglers? Or did they think he was a spy?

"Ye're weel turned oot for a clerk," continued McKie, eying Tom's coat. Behind them, Mungo just about managed to suppress a giggle as McKie turned his attention back to the accounts.

"These seem tae be in order," he said eventually. "I congratulate ye, Mr Cunningham. Still, we need tae check the lists against the stock in the warehoose. Follow me, gentlemen."

Tom felt increasingly uneasy as they crossed the yard. As the most recent employee, and one who had hardly been allowed access to the warehouse since his first day, he was sure that if anything illegal was found Kennedy would make sure that suspicion fell on him.

The big double doors to the warehouse were flung open and once inside, the excise men walked carefully up and down the aisles, checking the stock lists against the rows of kegs of spirits, crates and bottles of wine and chests containing tea and spices. They worked methodically and as he walked behind them Tom found himself examining the warehouse through their eyes, alert to anything which might arouse suspicion.

When they reached the last aisle, furthest from the doors, the light was so dim that it was difficult to make out the contours of the tea chests piled high against the back wall. Gavin McKie called for light and Kennedy approached with a lantern, raising it high so that the excise men could count the chests.

"That seems tae be in order," said McKie, turning away. He paused, then turning back sharply he added, "Just one mair thing. Would ye be sae good as tae fetch a chest doon frae that top row and open it for me?"

"At yer service," muttered Kennedy.

A ladder was produced and Geordie McSkimming climbed

up nimbly and cursing, heaved a cumbersome chest down to the floor.

"An' if ye could just open it for me ..." continued McKie.

Tom saw Kennedy and Geordie exchange a glance before Kennedy shrugged, placed the lantern on the dusty floor and fetched a jemmy.

What will they find? wondered Tom, intrigued in spite of his apprehension.

The lid came off and the familiar musky scent of dried tea leaves filled the air.

"Maybe you gentlemen were expecting something else?" enquired Kennedy smoothly, with a barely concealed edge of contempt in his voice.

"No indeed," replied McKie, "but ye ken fine oor job is tae check. That will be a' for noo." He gestured to them to close the chest and turned away.

Tom supposed he had not really expected the chest to contain anything other than tea, but by the light of the lantern on the floor he had noticed something unusual. There were marks in the dust by the row of tea chests, marks which suggested that one whole block of them had been moved not long before. He quickly made a mental note of the position of the block before following the others out of the warehouse.

*

As the working day drew to a close, Tom found himself alone in the office. Mr Cunningham had already left and Mungo had been sent to start checking the cargo of a newly-arrived ship before going home. Glancing out of the window, he saw that the yard was deserted and the warehouse doors shut. It was his opportunity to search the stock and he had to take it, for he was unlikely to have another chance.

He quickly tidied his desk, crossed to the inner office which Mr Cunningham usually left unlocked, and approached the desk. He half hoped to find it locked, being apprehensive about what he was about to do, but the drawer opened smoothly to reveal Mr Cunningham's keys. Tom quickly pocketed them, closed the drawer and both office doors, then he was down the steps and across the yard to the small side entrance to the warehouse before he could change his mind.

After fumbling with a few keys he found the right one. The door creaked loudly as he opened it and stepped into the gloomy interior. He stopped to let his eyes adjust to the dim light, aware of the pounding of his heart as he moved between the towering rows of goods, half expecting Kennedy or one of the McSkimmings to pounce on him. But the warehouse was deserted and soon he was standing by the row of chests along the back wall.

His eyes were now accustomed to the evening sunlight shining through the high windows and he soon found the block of chests he had noticed earlier. They were piled three high, and Tom wondered if he would be able to move them. He found the ladder which had been used that morning, propped it against the chests and climbed quickly. He grasped the sides of the topmost chest, expecting it to be very heavy, but to his surprise it weighed very little and he was able to lower it to the floor without difficulty. The second chest followed, then he climbed back down from the ladder and grasped the bottom chest, which also moved easily. All three were empty, or very nearly. Tom glanced at the bare wall where the chests had been and dimly made out the outline of a door.

"Probably locked," he thought, but he tried it anyway. He drew back the heavy bolt and the door swung open. Behind was thick darkness, but he could just make out some stone steps leading downwards into the gloom. He fetched the lantern Kennedy had used earlier and managed to light it with a taper from the embers of the fire in the brazier, then he went back to the door.

He could feel his heart pounding as he set off cautiously down the uneven steps, trying not to think of what might happen if he fell, or if Kennedy or the warehousemen came back. If they were up to something, and it seemed likely that they were, they wouldn't leave the place unguarded for long.

At the bottom of the steps Tom found himself in a dark cellar. Some light did come in from two small grimy windows high in the walls, which he judged must be at street level. Raising the lantern to examine his surroundings, Tom let out a low whistle. Kegs and crates of wines and spirits were piled neatly all around three walls, and in the centre stood piles of chests like those in the warehouse above. Some were open and on closer inspection proved to contain, not tea, but coffee, spices, fine china and bolts of Indian silk. Rather incongruously, he found himself wondering what Alison Fleming could do with such beautiful material.

He had obviously found what he was looking for; evidence that Cunningham's firm was engaged in smuggling. But who exactly was doing it? Was Richard Cunningham himself involved? Where did these goods come from and where did they go? Tom's thoughts were in a whirl and he felt fear clutch at his heart.

Just then he heard a muttered curse from above, followed immediately by footsteps on the stairs. There was nothing he could do; he was holding a lantern and it was too late to hide, so he stood rooted to the spot, feeling daft.

"What the ... Tom!"

"Mungo!"

The two young men stood, eyeing each other suspiciously. Mungo recovered first.

"Are you ...?"

"No ... you?"

"Naw, I'm nae smuggler, but I've kent for a while something was up. Put that licht oot, somebody might see in."

Tom was unsure whether to trust Mungo, but he saw the sense of this. Reluctantly, he extinguished the light. While his eyes were still adjusting to the gloom Mungo grasped his arm, making him jump.

"What are ye, feart? It's Kennedy and the McSkimmings, I'm sure o' that noo. Ye saw how they chose a full chest tae show the excise men, an' they must use the empty chests tae hide the door, but be able tae get in tae the cellar easily." He stopped and looked suspiciously at Tom. "How did ye ken whaur tae look?"

"I saw some marks in the dust and guessed they must move the chests there round a lot. I thocht there must be something behind them, but I never guessed there was a whole cellar doon here."

"I did," said Mungo proudly, "but I wasnae sure till the noo how tae get intae it frae the warehoose. There's anither way in frae the street." He pointed to the wall where the windows were, then pushed aside a couple of tall chests to reveal a low door.

"If ye gang intae the back alley ahint the warehouse," he said, "ye can see thae windows. There's some barrels on the street side tae hide the door, but I'm no fooled. That's where they bring the stuff in an' oot, so it never gangs through the books. Must be."

"When dae they dae it?" asked Tom.

"Must be at nicht. These summer nichts, it'll be gye late, and in ony case it has tae be when it's dark and folks are asleep, an' between the rounds o' the watch. It's weel organised, richt enough."

"So wha's daein' it? If it's the warehoosemen, they must never sleep."

"Aye, the McSkimmings look like they're sleepwalkin', whiles." Mungo grinned. "They'll be involved, all right. My guess is they're workin' wi a gang o' ne'er-dae-weels, outlaws, gypsies an' the like. There's plenty o' them roamin' the countryside. Adam Kennedy leaves this door unlocked and the gang come an' go as they like. I'd guess Kennedy gets weel paid for his trouble but mair than likely they're a' cheatin' on yin anither. It's a dangerous game, an' nae mistake."

"An' you seem tae ken a' aboot it," thought Tom. He felt sick with foreboding. He looked round the cellar again, at the wealth of goods it contained.

"Whaur does the stuff come frae?" he asked. "It disnae come in on the regular ships, surely?"

"Comes frae a' ower," said Mungo. "There's a lot o' it goes on, a' up and doon the coast. It comes in on wee ships frae France, Ireland, a lot by way o' the Isle o' Man, an' they land it a' doon the Carrick shore an' on the Solway coast as weel."

"But whaur does it gang frae here? Wha buys it?"

"Glasgow, Edinburgh, England. There's a lot o' folk wi' money, an' money maks ye greedy. Yon fine lords an' ladies aye hae an eye oot for a bargain, aye, an' yer fancy lawyers tae," he added with a sly glance at Tom. "The merchants that sell them their fine wines an' silks an' china are no' gonnae speir if the duty's been paid on them. I wouldnae be surprised if stuff frae the cellar here gangs oot wi' the regular carts in the daytime an' a'. There'll be false bottoms on the carts tae hide a' sorts o' stuff that never gangs through the books. You an' I can be as carefu' as we can wi' the invoices an' the accounts, but there's goods we never see, maybe even mair nor the legitimate stock."

"Ye seem tae ken a' aboot it," said Tom. "What are ye gaun tae dae?

"Dae?" scoffed Mungo. "Nothin', I suppose. Yon gypsies would slit your throat soon as look at ye, the McSkimmings an' a'. They're in it up tae their necks an' they've ower much tae lose. I dinnae want tae stir up this hornets' nest, but I cannae help wonderin' just what goes on." He looked slyly at Tom again. "What aboot you?"

"Dae ye think Mr Cunningham kens?"

"Honestly, I've nae idea. He seems the model upright citizen, but ye never ken. I must admit I'm curious though, noo that we've found the goods. Are you no'?"

"Aye, but what can we dae? It seems ower dangerous, from what ye say."

"Maybe best tae dae nothin', then," sighed Mungo. "The less we ken, the better, maybe . . ." He sounded as if he were trying to convince himself, and Tom too felt reluctant to do nothing with his new-found knowledge, in spite of the danger.

Mungo turned back towards the stairs. "Think on it. Maybe we could find oot mair, an' we can aye stop if it gets dangerous. I'll awa' noo. Mind ye put the chests back an' lock up. I'll see ye the morn." His footsteps grew fainter as he climbed the stairs and crossed the warehouse, leaving Tom alone in the dark.

He thought over what they had found. The sheer amount of goods in the gloomy cellar suggested it was a big operation, and surely he was putting his life in danger if he tried to find out more, but he couldn't help being curious. Realising that the door to the warehouse was still open and that he could be discovered at any time, he groped his way up the uneven steps, shut and bolted the door behind him and set about replacing the tea chests. He saw that there were now considerably more marks on the dusty floor but his efforts to smooth them over only seemed to make things worse. He just hoped no-one would notice.

Before going home, Tom led Sadie round to the alley which ran along the back of the warehouse. Sure enough, the street here was at a lower level than at the front and in the gathering twilight he could easily make out the two small cellar windows. A pile of barrels (empty, Tom suspected) hid the low door. He felt again the sick sense of foreboding and, shivering in the damp evening air, set off for home.

CHAPTER 9

Tuesday August 21st

———————

The next day was one of the strangest Tom had experienced at Cunningham's. There was an almost carnival atmosphere of relief at having survived the visit of the excise men. The McSkimming brothers were in high spirits, whistling and joking as they rolled barrels across the yard, singing lustily as they heaved crates on to the carts. Adam Kennedy moved with an even more pronounced swagger than usual and directed an openly contemptuous sneer at Tom when he went to collect the stock lists for the latest shipments.

Mungo seemed nervous, as if fearing he had revealed too much to Tom of what he suspected. There was still only tentative trust between them. Mr Cunningham, quietly sober as usual but obviously pleased at the outcome of the inspection, gave everyone a free afternoon, and Tom was glad to make his escape.

As he stabled Sadie at Barnessie House he noticed a small grey donkey placidly munching oats in the next stall. Entering through the kitchen as usual he found Bob, up to his elbows in flour and sneezing profusely, who told him that the donkey belonged to "yon wee seamstress". Tom remembered that Alison had promised to measure his mother for a new gown. He was surprised to find himself looking forward to sparring with her again.

In the sitting room he found his mother, Alison and Kate on the sofa together, among the remains of tea things, poring over fashion magazines. Engrossed in their discussion, they did not hear him come in.

"So maybe this yin wi' the new higher waist and a lace inset?" asked Alison.

"In a nice silk brocade," added Kate. "What colour are ye thinkin' of, mither?"

"It'll be Mistress Fleming's usual puce, if it's no' acid green," said Tom from the doorway.

All three looked up and Lady Margaret frowned.

"Thomas, you are an exceedingly rude young man. Mistress Fleming is oor guest; please greet her properly."

"Guid day tae ye, Mistress Fleming," muttered Tom.

"And tae you, sir." Alison turned back to Lady Margaret. "I was thinking o' a shade somewhere between grey and blue."

"Oh yes," breathed Kate, looking at Alison with undisguised admiration.

"Ye'll be sayin' next ye want tae be a seamstress when ye grow up," said Tom. "Is there ony tea in the pot?"

"That will be fine, if she's as talented as Mistress Fleming," said his mother. "I'm looking forward tae having a new gown. Now, Tom, tell us aboot yer day. How is Mr Cunningham?"

"Very well," said Tom, lowering his lanky frame into an armchair and helping himself to a large piece of shortbread. "He's pleased the excise men hae gone." Tom had not told his family about the previous day's discoveries; he had not yet decided what, if anything, to do about them.

"How's Mungo?" asked the ever-inquisitive Kate.

"Mungo?" asked Alison sharply.

"Aye," said Kate. "Mungo McGillivray, Tom's workmate – and new best friend," she added slyly. "He's got red hair and a temper."

"Kate," said her mother. "Ye mustn't speak ill o' people, especially those ye dinnae ken. Surely ye hae some school work tae finish?"

"I've done it a'," said Kate demurely.

"Mungo?" repeated Alison. "Forgive me, but I might ken his family. Do you?"

Tom stretched out his legs lazily and took another bite of shortbread.

"I doubt ye'd ken his family," he said. "His mither's a puir auld drunken wifie. Paisley Annie, they cry her."

"On the contrary," said Alison, fixing Tom with a hostile stare. "I ken Annie quite weel. I've visited her a few times an' if ye're friendly wi' her son ye might ask him why, when he earns a guid living, he neglects her to the point where she has neither food nor fire."

"He says if he gi'es his mither money she spends it on drink, then she's incapable for the rest o' the day."

"So he shirks a' responsibility for her an' leaves her tae stew in her ain filth. What kind o' a son does that?" demanded Alison furiously.

"Maybe there are reasons we dinnae ken."

"Aye, maybe so," said Alison sarcastically.

There was a heavy silence while Tom and Alison glared at each other. At length Alison said. "Please forgive me, ma'am. I forgot I am your guest. Now if ye'll excuse me, it's getting late and I must see tae my faither. I'll call again wi' some designs an' fabric samples, if that's convenient."

A meeting was arranged for the following week, and after thanking Lady Margaret for her hospitality, Alison took her leave. Tom was ordered to remember his manners and accompany her downstairs.

They descended the broad staircase in silence. By the front door Tom said, "Ye're wrong aboot Mungo, ye ken."

"I ken what I've seen in their hame. Nae son worth the name would treat his mither so."

"Then we'll hae tae agree tae differ," said Tom stiffly.

For a long moment, they stared at each other, then Alison said, "I'll find my ain way tae the stables. Guid day tae ye, Master Tom." She turned away quickly and Tom could only watch her slim, dignified figure as she crossed the yard.

Back upstairs, he was lectured once again on his rudeness by his mother, and reflected ruefully that he probably deserved it.

*

Steady rain and cold, unseasonal winds over the following days kept good burghers indoors and made farmers increasingly fearful for the coming harvest. Tom continued to brood about the smuggling question, telling himself he needed to find more evidence but using the bad weather as a convenient excuse for doing nothing. He had not spoken to his family about it and the inclement weather did nothing to lighten the heavy sense of foreboding he felt.

On Thursday, Mungo took him aside as they finished work and told him he had overheard a conversation between Adam Kennedy and Geordie McSkimming.

"They said Friday, midnight, at Culzean," he said with barely concealed excitement. "I've a mind tae gang an' see what they're aboot. What dae ye say? Will ye come wi' me?"

Tom hesitated. It could be a trap. Mungo had always given the impression of being reluctant to get involved, so why was he so keen to spy on Kennedy now? Still, Tom wanted to know what was going on and this would certainly give him an opportunity.

"What are ye plannin' tae dae?" he asked warily.

"We wait till it's dark, ride doon tae Culzean and see what's goin' on. There'll be naebody else aboot an' it'll be easy tae hide. We can maybe even follow them efterwards."

"But what if they discover us?"

"That's a risk we'd have tae take. We can aye say we want tae join wi' them."

Tom thought it would be unlikely the smugglers would believe that. If he went along with Mungo he would be getting into deeper water, but it was better than not knowing what was going on and doing nothing.

"Very well, then," he said. "I'll dae it."

Mungo's face brightened. "Guid man," he said. "I'll meet ye the morn's nicht at Alloway Kirk at ten o'clock. That'll gie us time tae get tae Culzean afore them."

CHAPTER 10

Friday August 24th

Getting to Alloway the following evening proved not to be as easy as Tom had thought. His parents allowed him to come and go as he pleased, but they would wonder at his leaving the house so late, and he had reckoned without the family's supper guests, the Misses McFadzean. They arrived at seven o'clock and settled down for an evening's gossip around the supper table.

The talk ranged widely and eventually turned to the American war, which was now going badly for the British, and on which the Misses McFadzean felt qualified to make informed comments. Miss Effie: "We should hae kent better than tae trust onybody ca'ed Washington – an arrant scoundrel." Miss Letty: "And that Jefferson wi' his new-fangled ideas – liberty, indeed!"

None of the family felt equal to the task of engaging the aunts in a prolonged political discussion and talk soon turned to matters nearer home and to the plight of the unfortunate Bessie Gibney. Miss Effie: "The lassie only has hersel' tae blame; she's nothing but a wanton hussy." Miss Letty: "Thank goodness we hae the Kirk Session tae stamp oot fornication," – this last with a pointed look at Tom, whose supposed Parisian misdemeanours had still not been forgotten.

Tom felt increasingly ill at ease. He had met many in France who admired Jefferson and Lafayette, and he remembered how uncomfortable he'd felt during Bessie's punishment in the kirk. Added to that, it was gone half past nine, darkness was starting to close in, his aunts showed no sign of leaving and he was going to be late for his appointment with Mungo.

"You're fidgeting a lot, Tom," observed his mother. "Are ye feelin' all right?"

Tom seized the opportunity. "It's true I dinnae feel sae weel," he said. "Might be the pie. If ye'll excuse me, I'll just gang oot for some fresh air and then turn in." He said his farewells to his aunts and beat a hasty retreat, silently blessing Jeanie and her lack of cooking skill.

The sky was clear and the moon just coming out as he fetched Sadie from the stable and walked her quietly out of the yard, then mounted quickly and galloped off towards Alloway.

He dismounted some distance from the kirk and approached it quietly, leading Sadie and wondering where Mungo was. The moonlight picked out the gaping windows and moss-covered stones of the old ruined church, the trees rustled eerily in the night air and somewhere a lone owl called.

"Feart o' houlets, are ye?" came a mocking voice from somewhere nearby.

Tom nearly jumped out of his skin but sighed with relief as Mungo approached from among the trees, saying "Ye took yer time, man. I thocht ye werenae comin'."

"Sorry," muttered Tom. "What noo?"

"We'll just hae time tae get tae Culzean an' hide afore they come. I'll need tae tak it easy; I'm no' ower sure o' this nag," he added, indicating a mangy-looking horse he had borrowed from the livery stable in Ayr.

Nonetheless, they made good progress down the lonely inland road towards Culzean, riding as silently as they could through the moonlit fields. When they arrived near the tall walls of the new building, Mungo signalled to Tom to dismount.

"There's a wee yard ower there where we can leave the horses. The yett's aye open and naebody gangs there, so they'll be safe."

He's done this before, thought Tom, fearing again that this was a trap, but he dismounted and followed Mungo through the narrow gate. After tethering the horses they followed a path down to the clifftop and settled down among some gorse bushes to wait.

The moonlight traced a bright silver path over the waters of the Firth, and the only sounds were the light rustle of the wind in the trees and the rhythmic sighing of the waves on the shingles beneath them.

"There's nothin' here," said Tom.

"Maybe they'll no' come if the moon's ower bricht," began Mungo, then broke off and clutched Tom's arm. "Ower there!" he hissed.

Looking in the direction Mungo indicated, Tom could just make out the bulky outline of a ship, lying at anchor off to the right in the murky darkness about five hundred yards from the shore.

"See?" Mungo couldn't keep the excitement from his voice. "Just wait, it'll a' be happenin' soon."

Tom could contain his curiosity no longer.

"I need tae ask ye, Mungo. Hoo come ye ken sae much aboot this?"

"I just listen tae what folks say. I've aye thocht there'd be smuggling somewhere at Cunningham's; it would be odd if there wasnae. I've been watchin' Kennedy an' the McSkimmings for a while ..."

"Aye, ye tellt me that afore. Hoo did ye ken whaur tae come the nicht?"

"Like I said, I heard them talkin'."

"But ye ken the lie o' the land an' whaur tae hide the horses."

Mungo was silent for a while. Finally he said, "I did come here once afore. I saw Kennedy in The Plough in the High Street and followed him when he left. Sure enough, he met up wi' Wullie an' Geordie an' they came doon here. I managed tae follow them."

"On foot?" asked Tom. "It's mair nor ten miles."

"I borrowed a horse frae the inn yard. No' officially, ye understand, an' I put it back efter. Naebody was ony the wiser."

In spite of himself, Tom had to smile, but he realised that Mungo's curiosity had led him to take a big risk. The law wasn't kind to horse thieves.

"Look," went on Mungo. "If ye think I'm involved, ye're wrang. Why would I tell ye a' this if I was?"

While this might be true, Tom was only half convinced.

"Wheesht noo," hissed Mungo. "There's folk comin'."

As they watched, a shadowy group of figures emerged from up by the castle and walked down towards the cliff edge. Tom held his breath as the men passed near their hiding place, and nearly shouted out as the leading figure turned his head in their direction and the moonlight picked out the scarred features of Adam Kennedy. Mungo clutched his arm warningly and Tom felt his heart pounding against his ribs.

Kennedy paused for a moment, looking round, and Tom felt the jagged gorse dig into his thighs as he tried to duck even further down. Then Kennedy and his companions disappeared down a cliff path and Tom heaved a great sigh of relief. He could feel Mungo trembling beside him.

A short while later the faint sound of tramping feet and muttered conversations drifted up from the beach; Kennedy and his crew had obviously been joined by others.

"Wha are they?" whispered Tom.

"Local folks, cottars an' the like. If they join in, they get a share o' the spoils. If they dinnae ... weel, onything can happen." Tom shivered, thinking of Kennedy and the McSkimmings' ruthless ways and remembering Mungo's tales of murderous clans of gypsies.

Suddenly Mungo clutched his arm, making him jump.

"Ye're awfu' nervous!" he sneered. "Look!"

Far below, they could see the glow of lanterns on the shore and then, from the hulk of the ship out in the firth, an answering light which blinked three times, then was extinguished.

"It's the signal!" said Mungo excitedly. "They'll put the boats oot noo."

Sure enough, they heard the scrape of small craft being hauled over the shingle and soon they saw half a dozen small boats being rowed across the moonlit water to the shadowed bulk of the ship. For the next hour or so they watched as kegs, crates and chests were ferried ashore and hauled with much panting and cursing up the steep cliff path.

Tom, still afraid that their hiding place might be discovered at any moment, did his best to ignore the creeping cold and numbness in his limbs, to which was now added an overwhelming need to pee, and tried to concentrate on what the crates and chests might contain. Spirits, he thought, wine, tea, silks and salt, much as he had seen in the hidden cellar at Cunningham's. In spite of himself, he was impressed by the speed and efficiency of the operation.

Eventually Mungo whispered, "Seen enough? We should gang noo, while they're still maistly doon on the shore."

"Are we no' gonnae follow them?"

"No' this time. We ken whaur maist o' the stuff's gaun."

Stiff and sore from lying in the gorse, Tom scrambled to his feet, stretched painfully and followed Mungo in a crouching run back up to the yard where they had left the horses.

"Wait, Mungo," called Tom. "I need tae piss."

Mungo cast his eyes heavenwards and hopped in exasperation as Tom relieved himself.

"Come on quick, noo."

They freed the horses quickly and began to lead them out of the yard as noiselessly as possible, but as they rounded the corner they came face to face with Adam Kennedy. Recognition on both sides was instant.

The next moment of silence seemed like an eternity before Kennedy spoke, in a voice dripping with scorn.

"Weel, weel. The carroty gowk an' the fancy fake Frenchie."

They said nothing, just stood rooted to the spot as Kennedy, hands on hips, slowly looked them up and down.

Finally he said, "Ye're lucky I havenae time tae deal wi' ye the noo, but we ken whaur tae find ye, an' we will."

The moonlight picked out the livid scar on his face as he slowly drew his finger across his throat and his mocking laughter followed them as they scrambled on to their horses and galloped off down to the road.

When they had gone some way and were sure no-one was following them they reined in. Tom leaned on his saddlebow, breathing hard, and looked over at his companion. Mungo, all bravado gone, was white and shaking.

"We're done for," he whispered hoarsely. "They'll kill us."

Tom thought fast. "Maybe no'," he said. "He could hae ca'd the ithers an' done it then if he had a mind. Maybe he doesnae dare. Folk would want tae ken why if we turned up deid."

"You, maybe," said Mungo bitterly. "Naebody would care aboot me."

Tom silently acknowledged that this was unfortunately likely to be true.

"There's your mither," he said, and as Mungo did not reply, he went on, "For noo, we should just wait an' see. Kennedy disnae ken what we're gonnae dae, an' that'll mak' him uneasy. Maybe he'll offer tae let us in on it."

"That's no' likely," jeered Mungo. "Less profit for them. No, if he had a mind tae it, he could gey soon mak' us disappear."

"So we'll stick thegither a' the time we're at work, an' we dinnae gang intae the warehoose alone."

"Work? I dinnae want tae gang near Cunningham's again, no' efter this."

"But can ye no' see, it's safer there, whaur we can see what's goin' on, an' if we aye stick thegither, they cannae trap us in a corner."

"They can follow us hame."

"I dinnae think they'd risk onything in broad daylight when there's folk aboot. We'll just need tae watch oor backs. Come on noo, let's get hame afore they come."

Sure enough, there were no immediate repercussions. They parted at Barnessie House, Mungo declining Tom's offer of a bed for the night saying "How would ye explain it tae yer ma? She doesnae ken ye're oot."

Tom sighed as he watched him trot off down the road on his borrowed nag. He would never get used to Mungo's sudden changes of mood.

The house was in darkness; none of the family had noticed Tom's absence. Safe in his room, he reflected that at least he was sure now that Mungo was not involved with the smugglers.

Work on Saturday passed off without incident. Mr Cunningham had them working hard on the thorough revision of all accounts which he undertook once a year, and although they saw Kennedy and the warehousemen in the yard, looking carefree and unconcerned, no-one came near the office. Both Mungo and Tom were glad to leave at three.

At the card table after supper, looking at the cheerful faces of his family and listening to his father discoursing on the latest items of interest from the Scots Magazine, Tom began to relax. The events of the previous night began to seem like a bad dream.

"Aye, Monboddo's a queer gowk a' right, for a' he's a fellow member o' the judiciary." Sir Malcolm was saying. "He thinks apes resemble humans. He'll be saying next we're related tae them. Mind ye, when ye see hoo Bob walks, ye can see why."

Tom smiled. He wouldn't be repeating that to Bob.

CHAPTER 11

Sunday August 26th

———

Alison Fleming hummed to herself as she worked at the big table in the back room of the shop. Her father had gone to Glasgow on the Friday to buy cloth and Alison had become absorbed in designing Lady Margaret's new gown. In front of her on the table were four different sketches and some scraps of grey and blue silk and brocade. It was Sunday, but as it was pouring with rain again and especially as she had no wish to see the further humiliation of Bessie Gibney, she had decided not to go to church, hoping that folk would assume she had gone to Glasgow with her father.

As she picked up and discarded various scraps of lace and ribbon, trying to decide on suitable trimmings, Alison realised that she had seldom enjoyed a task so much. She had loved her visit to Barnessie House, talking to gentle Lady Margaret and her spirited daughter, pleased that they had taken such an obvious and genuine interest in her work. "Great folk, the Boyd family," she reflected, "except perhaps the second son." She had to concede though that he was a well set-up young man and that she had enjoyed sparring with him. She wondered about his friendship with Mungo McGillivray; it had shocked her that Tom had leapt to his defence so easily, but she had to admit that he was loyal to his friend. Moreover, her regular visits to Annie had maybe improved Mungo's mother's material comfort, but her sober moments were still few.

So absorbed was she in her task that she did not hear the front door open and footsteps cross to the back shop. She started in fright as a deep, cracked voice boomed "Mistress Fleming! What in the name o' a' that's holy are ye daein'?"

Framed in the doorway stood the tall black-clad figure of James Cunningham, elder of the kirk. Alison got to her feet, striving with all her might to retain a calm and dignified demeanour, but her legs were shaking and she had to hold on to the edge of the table for support.

"I . . . meant nae harm, sir," she stammered.

"Nae harm! Ye were missin' at the kirk the day an' when I come oot o' Christian charity tae speir efter yer well-being, what dae I find? Ye're workin', ye're engaged in trade on the Lord's Day. We'll see what the Session has tae say aboot that, my lass."

Alison paled as she pictured herself, clad in sackcloth, standing on the stool in front of the congregation. Failure to observe the Sabbath might not quite rank with fornication as a crime in the eyes of the kirk elders, but she was in trouble none the less. She thought quickly.

"I didnae come tae the service as I was expecting my faither back frae Glasgow" – this was partly true, at least, – "an' forbye, I'm no *engaged in trade*" – she managed a faintly sarcastic tone of voice – "this gown is for mysel'."

Cunningham sighed deeply, and in the sorrowful tones of a judge explaining to a cattle thief that the law is the law and that regretfully he is going to have to hang him, said, "That's nae excuse for failure tae attend the kirk. And what's mair, ye've just added lying tae yer list o' sins. Thon are obviously samples and sketches intended for a customer – a *paying* customer. It cannae be helped, my lassie, ye'll have tae answer tae the Session." Then, as Alison stared at him, horrified, his tone changed. "That is, unless we can come tae an arrangement."

"An arrangement?" Alison repeated blankly, then, as Cunningham came round the table towards her, she began to see what he was hinting at. There was a wild light in his eyes and a mocking smile on his thin lips as he said "Ye're a weel-favoured lass an' if ye were willin' tae dae me a few wee favours I could put work yer way."

"So I could work every day, even on the Sabbath?" replied Alison with more bravado than she felt. "I don't think so, sir."

"Aye, ye've got spirit. I like that in a lass . . . tae an extent."

Before she could reply he took two steps towards her, grasped her arms and pinned her back against the wall. His face was just inches from hers and she could feel his hot breath, reeking of onions. "Come on," he said, "be nice tae me. I'm sure ye can." And then his thin, cruel mouth was fastened on hers. Alison jerked her head this way and that but he was too strong. She could feel the hardness as his body pressed close to hers, and in desperation she instinctively brought her knee up hard, into his groin. He let go with a curse but immediately came after her again, his face a mask of fury. Alison cried out as he grabbed her once more, clamped one hand over her mouth and with the other roughly seized the front of her gown and tore it from neck to waist.

*

Tom Boyd paced along the Sandgate in the wind and driving rain, in a foul mood. An after-church family gathering at the McFadzean aunts' house had turned out badly. Fear and worry over the smuggling, compounded by an unexpected stab of disappointment and concern he had felt on not seeing Alison in the kirk, had caused him to lose patience with his aunts' constant carping and pleading a headache, ("I'm concerned about that boy's health," "I blame the French,") he sought refuge in the rainy streets. Curiosity guided his steps towards the Flemings' shop, and as he neared the door he heard a scream from inside.

Tom didn't hesitate. He shouldered his way through the open shop door, skidded round the tailor's dummy, which miraculously stayed upright, and rushed into the workroom. He had just time to register Alison's shocked, pallid face and torn shift before launching himself at the black-clad figure hunched over her.

The two men grappled together. They were evenly matched

in strength, but Tom had been trained as a youngster by Bob in the art of fist-fighting and was able to land a cracking punch on his opponent's jaw. The man reeled back against the opposite wall and before he could move Tom had him pinned to the wall, one hand on his chest, the other at his throat. Somehow, he was not surprised to recognise James Cunningham.

"What's the meaning o' this?" he shouted.

"Let go of me and I will explain," said Cunningham coldly. He had regained his composure remarkably quickly. Tom reluctantly lowered his hands.

"Seeing Mistress Fleming and her faither were missing frae the service this morning, I came to enquire after their welfare and I found this young lady" – his voiced dripped with sarcasm – "engaged in profit-making business on the Lord's Day. I informed her that she would be called to account by the Kirk Session, whereupon the brazen jade attempted to turn me away frae my purpose wi' her wicked wiles."

Alison gasped, and one glance at her shocked face confirmed to Tom where the truth lay.

"That's no' what I saw," he said angrily, "an' I heard her scream frae ootside. It's plain tae me ye've tried tae take advantage o' an innocent lassie. It's you who should have tae answer for it."

"I doubt if your word would be believed against mine. I am elder o' the kirk, dinnae forget."

"Aye," said Tom bitterly, "an' nae doot ye consider yersel' one o' the elect. Ye're convinced ye hae eternal salvation and that gi'es ye licence tae dae as ye like. But I ken what I hae seen here and nae power on heaven or earth can excuse it. You threatened an' took advantage o' a defenceless woman and make no mistake, the Session will hear o' this."

"Ha!" spat Cunningham. "Ye think they'll believe you, after a' I've heard o' your reputation? Fornicator!"

And with that he turned and made for the door.

"Mr Cunningham?" came Alison's voice, shaky but determined.

He stopped, one hand on the latch, and turned to glare at her.

"Wha's the faither o' Bessie Gibney's bairn?"

Cunningham stood for a moment, speechless with rage, then with a muttered curse he was away.

Alison gripped the edge of the table.

"Forgive me, I need tae sit doon," and she stumbled to a chair, clutching at the edges of her torn clothing. She was shaking uncontrollably and Tom saw tears of shame and anger in her eyes.

He fetched a shawl from the shop and a small tot of whisky from the kitchen press. She accepted both gratefully and gradually, as Tom looked on anxiously, some colour returned to her cheeks.

"Can ye tell me what happened?" he asked gently.

Alison drew a heavy sigh, then explained haltingly. Finally, "It was a guid thing ye came by when ye did," she said with a shudder as she pictured what might have happened. "Thank you."

"How are ye feeling?"

She managed a shaky smile. "A bit better. I'll be fine in a minute."

They sat in awkward silence for a minute or so, then Tom asked, "What was that aboot Bessie Gibney?"

Alison shrugged, "Nothin' much. I just thocht he might ken something, that's a'."

"Forgive me, but there's mair than that, the way ye speired. Come on, ye can trust me."

"Aye, that I can." Alison looked at him steadily, then went on, "It was last Sunday in the kirk. When they made Bessie stand. I was watching Cunningham. He looked pleased, but it was mair than that. He was fair gloatin'."

"Aye, I saw that. He was ower pleased wi' himsel'." A thought struck him. "Dae ye think he's the wean's faither?"

"I've nae notion. But if he's no', he kens wha is. An' if he is the faither, Bessie's too feart tae name him, so we'd never prove it. I've aye thocht there was somethin' o' the justified sinner aboot him."

"Aye, he thinks he's one o' the elect, so he can be as wicked as he likes and it'll mak' nae difference at the Day o' Judgment."

"He's a hypocrite, aye preachin' at ithers, but whaur's his Christian charity?" Alison shivered. "I'm just feart he'll come back. Faither's no' due hame till the morn."

"Ye could come tae Barnessie wi' me," offered Tom.

Alison gave him a wan smile.

"Ye're kind, but no. If we're seen leavin' here thegither, we'll baith be up before the Session, especially wi' your reputation. In fact, ye'd best gang oot the back way."

Tom grinned ruefully. "Oh aye, it seems I'm the Great Fornicator. It's no' somethin' I've ever done." Suddenly he wanted Alison to believe him, very much.

"Don't worry Tom. Ye're a fine young man," she said with a smile. "Noo, awa' ye go, an' let me get on wi' breaking the Sabbath."

"Are ye sure ye'll be all right?"

"Aye. When I'm busy wi' my wark, I forget everything else."

"Just make sure ye keep the door bolted till yer faither comes hame."

"I will."

As Tom went off to join his family, he realised that in the space of two days he had made two dangerous enemies and one friend. There was no doubt that it was the latter who was more important to him and as he hurried along the Sandgate in the rain, his thoughts were full of Alison Fleming.

*

Alison spent the next day in an unaccustomed state of nerves. She had been badly shaken by her encounter with James Cunningham and only felt a little better when her father arrived back from Glasgow. For his part, he was surprised to be welcomed even more warmly than usual by his daughter and he had to tell her to stop fussing when she sat him in the armchair by the inglenook, drew off his boots and made sure his pipe and glass of whisky were to hand before sitting down opposite and questioning him at inordinate length about his trip.

"There's somethin' botherin' ye lassie," he said at last. "What's been happenin'?"

Alison coloured. "Naethin' much, faither. I think the stew's near ready," she continued, jumping up to stir the pot. Her father sighed, recognising that she would not be drawn any further.

CHAPTER 12

Tuesday August 28th

Alison stood at her work table, cutting orange taffeta for another gown for Miss Effie McFadzean, trying to concentrate on her task and ignore the constant reminders of the attack which had taken place in that very room two days before. Thank goodness Tom Boyd had come along when he did. Alison would not let herself think about what might have happened, but in spite of her fear she found herself smiling as she thought of Tom. He was far from the foolish young wastrel she had first thought him; he was brave and kind and she felt herself increasingly drawn to him. Not all men were like James Cunningham, and men of his sort would carry on their wicked ways as long as they could get away with it. "*Why* should *he get away with it?*" she thought, as an idea began to form in her head.

In the afternoon she went down to Mill Street to see Annie and was surprised to find the hearth swept and a small fire burning. Annie was brighter than usual. She had combed her hair and was sitting knitting by the fire. "Socks for Mungo," she said in answer to Alison's enquiry, "if I can mind how tae turn the heel." She proudly informed Alison that she hadn't had a drop of drink for two days and was determined to keep off the bottle. Looking round the dingy room Alison was pleased to see that Annie had made some attempt at cleaning. Perhaps now Mungo would spend more time at home and care better for his mother.

"Mungo brocht some tea frae the office," Annie said. "I'll brew us a cup, if ye like."

Alison accepted gratefully and soon the two women were chatting amicably. It turned out that Annie knew, or knew about, nearly everybody in Ayr.

"Dae ye ken Bessie Gibney?" asked Alison, who had thought a lot about that young woman over the previous days.

"Bessie Gibney ... aye, she's a washerwoman. She lives in a wee hut doon by the river wi' her wean, weans I suppose it'll be noo."

Alison had an idea. "Is it far frae here?" she asked.

"Ye gang along the bank towards the brig. It's aboot twa minutes' walk. She'll likely be workin' ootside the day as it's no' rainin'."

They talked for a few minutes more before Alison took her leave.

"Ye're lookin' a lot better, Annie," she said. "Thank ye for the tea."

As Alison made her way along the river bank in the direction Annie had indicated, she heard singing and laughter coming from up ahead, and rounding an overhanging hawthorn bush she saw two young women about her own age jumping up and down in big wooden wash tubs. Their sleeves were rolled up to reveal strong brown arms and coarse, reddened hands. They held their skirts clear of the water as their feet pounded the washing in the tubs. On the bushes all around sheets and shirts had been spread out to dry, some linen, some finer cambric. A plump, black-haired little girl of about two was playing in the mud by the water's edge and in a makeshift crib in the shade by the open hut door a baby was gurgling contentedly in its sleep.

Alison recognised the taller of the two women as Bessie Gibney and called out to her. She stopped jumping and stepped out of the tub, eying Alison suspiciously.

"What dae ye want, mistress?" asked Bessie.

"I dinnae think ye ken me. My name's Alison Fleming, frae the drapers in the Sandgate."

"Oh aye, I ken the place. I used tae work whiles for Mr Forsyth, that had the shop afore ye."

The implied reproach in her words prompted Alison to ask, "How's the business noo? Ye seem tae hae plenty tae dae."

"Aye, the day. We're gettin' a' we can done in the guid weather. It's no easy when it rains an' we hae tae work inside. What brings ye here, mistress?" she added.

Alison hesitated, unsure how to continue.

"I might hae some work for ye," she began. "We often hae bolts o' cloth that need laundering afore I can use them. And dae ye dae ironing?"

"Aye," said Bessie, "I dae a guid job, an' I'll no deny we could dae wi' mair customers, my sister an' I. That's her there, Lizzie." Bessie indicated the other girl who had spread a shirt out on a flat stone and was beating the water out of it with a wooden bat. Lizzie raised a hand briefly in greeting.

"When would ye want this work done, mistress?" asked Bessie, jumping back into the tub to resume her tramping.

Alison thought quickly. She had not intended to offer Bessie custom, and although it now seemed a good way to get to know her better, she was unsure what to ask for.

"I'll bring ye the linen we need laundered the morn, if that's all right. I'm no' sure how much there'll be."

"An' ye'll pay the goin' rate, I'm sure," said Bessie. "Noo suppose ye tell me the real reason for yer call."

"Real reason?"

"Aye, weel, it's no' a social call, an' it's plain tae me ye had nae thocht o' employin' me when ye ca'd my name," said Bessie shrewdly.

"Well," Alison hesitated. "I saw ye in the kirk . . ."

"So did a wheen o' ither folk," said Bessie bitterly. "I'm surprised ye'd gi'e me wark efter seein' my disgrace."

"I thocht ye were very brave, listenin' tae a' the minister had tae say."

Bessie grinned suddenly. "Ye'll need tae tell me what he said. I wasnae listenin'."

"I was disgusted," said Alison frankly. "Why does the Kirk Session aye punish the lassie an' the bairn's faither gangs free?"

"You tell me," said Bessie grimly.

"Maybe," said Alison slowly, "because the bairn's faither is a fine, upstanding citizen. Maybe he's a member o' the Session."

Bessie stopped tramping. "What dae ye ken?" she demanded.

"I think I can guess wha the faither is. Thon's a bonnie black-haired wee lassie," she continued, indicating the child playing by the water. "That'll be yer dochter, I suppose."

Bessie shot her a furious look.

"Ye'll no mak' me say a name," she warned. "He sees me an' the weans provided for."

"What if I tellt ye the same fine gentleman had attacked me?"

"An' what o' it? Ye'll no' be the last," said Bessie bitterly.

"An' he'll carry on if he's no' stopped. Dae ye want that? How mony mair puir lassies will he defile if he can get awa' wi' it?"

Bessie heaved herself out of the tub and came to stand close to Alison. A smell of coarse soap and lye came with her.

"Listen, if ye want tae gang tae the Session an' denounce him I cannae stop ye. You'll no be hurt by it; ye've got a guid livin' an' a faither tae provide for ye, but me an' the ither lassies in my position hae nothin'. I've already lost customers an' if James Cunningham didnae provide for me, my weans an' I would starve."

Not seeming to realise she that she'd just named her children's father, Bessie seized a washing bat and a shirt and began to beat it furiously. "Guid day tae ye, Mistress Fleming," she flung over her shoulder.

Well, at least she'd had her suspicions confirmed, thought Alison as she walked away. In truth she had expected no other reaction from Bessie, but she hoped still that she could bring the girl round.

CHAPTER 13

Wednesday August 29th

"Mind hoo ye go. This gangplank's gey slippy." Mungo turned to grin at Tom. It was Wednesday afternoon and they were about to board the *Demoiselle*, a French brig tied up at the quayside, to check Cunningham's section of the cargo before she set sail for Dublin. Richard Cunningham had told Mungo to show Tom this part of the job, saying he would soon get the hang of it; it was just a matter of checking the bill of lading against the goods in the hold.

Tom had been gradually feeling more relaxed since the weekend. He and Mungo made sure they stayed together during the working day and went straight home afterwards. Tom usually accompanied Mungo as far as Mill Street before mounting Sadie for the ride home. They had little contact with Kennedy and the McSkimmings, who usually kept to the warehouse or the yard.

If he had been thinking less of the smugglers it was because he found his thoughts turning increasingly to Alison. He wondered if she had recovered from James Cunningham's unwanted attentions. Natural diffidence and a reluctance to remind her of her ordeal had so far prevented him from going to see her, but now he thought she might conclude that he didn't care. He decided he would go round to the shop after work; he could always pretend he was on an errand from his aunts.

Following Mungo, he negotiated the steep gangplank safely and crossed the deck to the trapdoor leading down to the smaller of the two holds. The rickety ladder down into the darkness was steep, and he had to place his feet carefully. Once below, Mungo lit a lantern which hung from the rafters and they looked around. The ship's main cargo, linen, was stored in bales in the main hold. Cunningham's wines and spirits, bound for the tables of the Dublin gentry, were stored in this second one, whose walls were lined with crates and kegs bearing the firm's distinctive stamp.

Mungo read out the items from the lists while Tom checked the goods. He was a meticulous worker, so the process lasted longer than usual. He could sense Mungo's impatience, but he was determined to do the job properly. The dim interior of the hold did not help; the lantern's beam did not reach into the corners, and the only other light came from the open trapdoor and from one dirty porthole in the ship's side.

They were just finishing the last section of cargo when there came a shout from above. "Are youse in there, Boyd, McGillivray?" and looking up, they saw the leering face of Adam Kennedy framed in the opening.

"Aye," said Tom, trying to keep fear out of his voice.

"Twa rats in a trap," sneered Kennedy. Tom felt his legs turn to jelly. He had noticed when they came aboard that there was no-one else on the ship. The crew had not yet come aboard. Beside him, Mungo gave a soft moan of fear.

"An' twa ship's rats ye'll remain. She sails on the evening tide an' I doot the crew'll find ye afore Dublin. Bon voyage an' gi'e my love tae the colleens!" and with a mocking laugh Kennedy slammed the trapdoor shut and rammed home the two stout bolts. They heard his heavy footsteps cross the deck above their heads, then there was silence.

"What the de'il . . . ?" spluttered Mungo.

Tom stumbled up the ladder and pushed at the trapdoor, to no avail.

"Save yer breath," said Mungo gloomily. "We're trapped. Just like rats, richt enough."

"Can we no' alert the crew?"

"Ye heard what he said. They're no aboard yet. They aye get a' ready, then go for a last wee dram afore they sail."

Tom cursed, then seized the lantern from its hook and began to examine the dark corners of the hold.

"What are ye daein' noo?" asked Mungo wearily. "We're stuck till Dublin, an' then they'll put us in jail, if we dinnae starve first." He slumped down on a keg of whisky and closed his eyes.

"There must be anither way oot," said Tom, prowling with the lantern around the edges of the hold.

"Aye, mebbe in a cheap chapbook story, or *The Ballad of Thomas Boyd*. Leave it, Tom, there's nothin' tae be done."

Tom had arrived next to the porthole. Raising the lantern, he examined the edges of the grimy glass. He scratched at the wooden frame. "Maybe we could loosen the glass here, and if we can open it we can ca' tae folk on the quay."

"What, an' hae Kennedy come runnin' back?"

"He'd no' dare dae onything in daylight." Tom felt in his pockets. "I've nothin' I could use. Hae ye got a knife or ocht sharp?"

Mungo reluctantly produced a rather rusty penknife, and Tom set to work scraping at the wooden frame of the porthole. Mungo curled up on the floor and went to sleep.

Half an hour later, Tom had made little progress. The putty holding the glass had been applied well and Tom's efforts were slow, but he was sure that he would eventually be able to remove the glass. Just then he heard footsteps up above which signalled the return of the crew. He ran to the trapdoor and began pounding on it as hard as he could. To no avail; he soon realised that the muffled sounds he produced would not be heard. Shortly afterwards there came the sounds of shouted commands and running feet as the sails were raised. He could hear them cracking in the stiff breeze as the ship rocked at anchor then settled again.

Tom paused, realising that they were about to set sail.

He did not allow himself to panic. He roused Mungo and the two of them began to shout at the top of their lungs, while Tom hammered with all his might on the trapdoor.

All their efforts were in vain, and shortly afterwards the ship's timbers shuddered and creaked as she cast off from the quay. Mungo slumped in despair.

Tom nearly did likewise, but told himself if he could get the porthole loose there was still a chance. He set to work again with the penknife. Beyond the grimy glass he could see the warehouses on the quay slide past, then the bulk of Cromwell's fort in the gathering gloom. The ship lurched alarmingly as they reached the river mouth and swung to starboard, out into the Firth, heading south. As the following wind filled the sails she began to move faster.

Tom had given up all hope of attracting the crew's attention. Their only hope was to get off the ship and swim for land but he realised that if he could not open the porthole soon they would be too far out. Just then he felt the framework give way and the glass fell out. Tom felt the salty taste of spray on his face and breathed in the cold night air. He could just make out the dark outline of the shore, about two hundred yards away. He pulled a keg over to the side, and climbing up, gauged the width of the opening. It would be a tight squeeze but he reckoned he could just about wriggle through the narrow gap. It would be easier for Mungo, who was shorter and slighter. Fortunately, the porthole was not far above the waterline, so they would not have far to fall.

"What are ye daein'?" asked Mungo, joining him by the porthole.

"I think we can just aboot get through here an' swim ashore. We'll need tae dae it noo, or it'll be ower late."

"We cannae."

"Why? It's oor only chance, or we'll be too far out tae get tae the shore."

"But... Mungo hung his head, "I cannae swim."

Tom hadn't foreseen this. He did his best to reassure the other man. "It's all right. I'll haud ye up. It's no' that far, but we'll hae tae gang noo."

Mungo swallowed. Tom could see he was caught between his fear of the water and his fear of the unknown. Finally, "I'll try," he whispered.

Tom clasped his shoulder briefly. "Guid man. Trust me, I'll no' let ye doon. I dinnae think the tide has quite turned yet, so that'll push us towards the shore. Noo tak' aff yer boots," he added, bending to remove his own.

"They're my only pair," protested Mungo.

"I'll bring ye some mair frae hame. A jacket an' a', for we'll need tae tak' them aff tae."

Mungo grumbled a bit, but then did as he was asked. They stripped quickly to shirt and hose.

"Noo dae just as I dae, an' ye'll be fine."

Holding on to a beam above the porthole, Tom swung himself up from the keg and pushed his legs out of the gap. The angle was not good and he had to wriggle his shoulders quite a bit but soon he was through the opening and falling into the sea below. He gasped as he hit the water; the sea was colder than he had thought. He hoped he would have the strength to make it to the shore with the added burden of Mungo.

He treaded water and looked up towards the porthole. The ship was moving away fast and Tom knew it would soon be too late to catch his friend. "Come on, Mungo," he yelled. "Ye'll need tae come noo."

"Mebbe I'll tak' my chance in Dublin," called Mungo.

"Like hell ye will. Noo, or it's too late!"

Mungo's head disappeared from sight, and Tom was about to swim for shore alone, but then he glimpsed a pair of legs in the opening and moments later there was a splash and Mungo disappeared under water. He seemed to spend a long time under, and Tom cursed himself for leading him into danger, but just then the waters parted and Mungo's head appeared, coughing and spluttering. Cursing beneath his breath, Tom struck out towards him. It was heavy going through the swell in the wake of the ship and he could hardly see the other man.

"Mungo!" he yelled. "Move yer arms and legs. Try tae stay afloat, I'm comin'!"

Mungo began flailing about but Tom was still about fifteen yards away when he panicked again and his head disappeared below the waves. Tom treaded water and waited apprehensively. The next few seconds seemed like an eternity before Mungo surfaced again. Tom covered the distance between them as fast as he could, terrified that Mungo's panic had caused him to lose what little strength he had left.

A final desperate lunge brought him close just as Mungo's head was about to disappear for the last time.

"Weel done," he gasped as he turned on his back and hooked his arms under Mungo's shoulders. The other man continued to struggle until Tom hissed in his ear, "I've got ye, ye daft gowk. Lie still noo." With that, he struck out with the strongest strokes he could manage towards the shore, and Mungo gradually relaxed. Tom had guessed right about the tide; the waves carried them shorewards, but the water was freezing cold and Tom felt his strength failing. He doubted they would make it.

"Mungo," he gasped to the dead weight in his arms, "try tae kick wi' yer legs. That'll help us." Sure enough Mungo, more relaxed and confident now, began to kick out too, increasing their momentum.

Before too long they were stumbling up through the shingle to collapse on the shore, where they lay gasping and spluttering. As they regained their breath they began laughing with relief as they watched the stern lantern on the *Demoiselle* as it sailed on towards the Irish Sea.

"Sorry, Dublin," said Mungo. "Maybe I'll see ye one day."

Tom, already on his feet was looking at their surroundings. There were lights in nearby windows, so he guessed they were not too far out of town.

"We'll need tae get hame," he said. "We dinnae want tae catch the cauld, or worse." They were suddenly both aware of their soaked clothes and lack of footwear.

"Aye," said Mungo, "but it was rare, richt enough." He gave a hoot of laughter. "I cannae wait tae see Adam Kennedy's face the morn."

*

Tom arrived early at the warehouse the next day. He had woken not long after dawn, surprised to find that he was none the worse for wear after the previous evening's exertions. He had made it on foot to Barnessie and the walk had warded off the chill from his bones. Finding the house in darkness he had left a note for his parents and gone straight to bed, where he slept the sleep of the just. In the morning he had breakfasted before the family was up, fetched some boots and a jacket for Mungo, and set off on foot for Ayr. He knew this feeling of elation would not last, and was determined to enjoy it while he could.

He looked in on Sadie, whom he had left overnight in Cunningham's stables. He fed her some oats and changed her straw, then made for the offices. As he crossed the yard he saw Mungo enter through the big doors to the quay. Out of the corner of his eye he spied Adam Kennedy coming out of the warehouse. He called to Mungo.

"Morning, Mungo. Hoo are ye the day?"

"Guid morning, Tom. Guid day tae ye, Mister Kennedy. I'm fine. It's true what they say, swimming's guid for the constitution. Is it no', Tom?"

"It is that. I can really recommend it, Mr Kennedy. You should try it sometime."

"Soon," added Mungo, with a meaningful glance at Kennedy. Laughing, the two young men crossed the yard and mounted the stairs to the office, leaving Kennedy open-mouthed.

CHAPTER 14

Friday August 31st

By Friday, Mungo's mood had changed again ... "I cannae thole much mair o' this." It was early morning. Tom had found Mungo in the office, shaking with nerves.

"I havenae slept," he moaned. "I'm aye feart they're comin' after me."

Tom shared his fear, but tried to reassure him. "They'll no' try onything in daylight, or here at work, after Wednesday. Just try tae relax. We'll stick thegither a' day an' get stuck intae the books. That'll tak' oor minds off them."

"Aye, but what aboot after? I tell ye, I hardly made it in here for lookin' ower my shoother in the street. I see shapes in a' the shadows an' hear footsteps when there's naebody there."

Tom hesitated. That morning David had arranged to meet him after work at The Plough, the large coaching inn in the High Street. "There's somebody I'd like ye tae meet," he'd said. Tom was intrigued and glad of the distraction. He'd stabled Sadie at The Plough that morning, intending to collect her there before going home. He did not know how David and his friend would react; would they mind if he brought Mungo along?

On an impulse he said, "I'm meeting my brither in The Plough at six. Come wi' me if ye like. A wee dram'll dae ye guid."

"Aye, maybe." Mungo's troubled face relaxed. "Thank ye, Tom."

Just then Mr Cunningham appeared from the inner office. "Come awa' ben, lads," he said. "We've a wheen o' ledgers tae get through the day."

They worked hard all day, checking the year's accounts, only stopping briefly when Mr Cunningham sent out for pies and ale at midday. Through the window, Tom could see Kennedy and the warehousemen going about their work in the yard, never looking in the direction of the offices. Everything seemed normal.

Just after three o'clock they heard a heavy tread on the creaking stairs and Adam Kennedy put his head round the door. He greeted the two clerks civilly, made some remark about the cold, windy weather and laid the latest delivery notes on Mungo's desk before knocking on the door of the inner office. They could hear him talking and laughing with Mr Cunningham, though they couldn't make out what was being said. Five minutes later he was back. "See ye around, lads," he said with a grin as he stomped off down the stairs, leaving Tom and Mungo wondering what threat lay behind this cheerful farewell.

At six o'clock they closed the ledgers and stood up. "We're awa' noo, Mr Cunningham," called Mungo. Their employer came out of his office, wiping ink stains from his fingers.

"Aye, lads, ye've worked weel the day." He fished some coins from his pocket. "Awa' an' hae a drink on me."

"Are ye no' coming yersel?" asked Mungo.

"No, thank ye. I've found a few places where the figures dinnae add up. I'll stay and work on for a bit. Mrs Cunningham's coming in later."

"Guid nicht then, sir," said Tom as he headed for the stairs.

"Guid nicht. I'll see ye baith the morn's morn."

*

"I dinnae like it," said Mungo as they crossed the bridge. "What were Kennedy and Mr. Cunningham talkin' aboot? They sounded ower friendly tae me."

Tom had been wondering about this himself. He still could not shake off the suspicion that their employer knew all about the smuggling, and perhaps was involved. He was reluctant to share his fears with Mungo however; that would only make his friend more nervous and fearful than ever.

"Dinnae fash yersel' the noo," he said. "Let's hae a dram an' forget aboot it."

They could hear the babble of voices as they turned in off the High Street to The Plough. Inside, the evening's revelry was well under way, if not yet in full swing. As their eyes adjusted to the dim, smoky interior and their ears to the hubbub, Tom heard his brother's voice. "Tom! Ower here!" and they pushed their way over to where David and his companion sat in the inglenook by the fire, nursing tankards of tuppenny ale.

David called for more ale, greeted Mungo and introduced his friend, a handsome, stocky young man in his early twenties with large, expressive dark eyes, longish black hair and an inquisitive expression.

"This is Rab, Rab Burns. He farms wi' his faither oot at Lochlie. My brither Tom and his friend Mungo work at Cunningham's."

The four young men settled down for an evening's talk. After some initial exchanges about the weather, which they all agreed was potentially disastrous for the harvest, Rab turned to Tom.

"I hear ye were in Paris. Ye must hae seen some sights there. I envy ye, man. I've never been oot o' Ayrshire."

Tom reflected ruefully that all he seemed to have gained in Paris were a broken heart and a ruined reputation, but faced with Rab's enthusiasm he did his best to describe the ferment of ideas and the excitement of living in Paris.

"There's folk wi' ideas in France, right enough," he said, "but there's hardship there tae. The puir hae nothin', the bourgeois are bled dry wi' taxes and the aristocrats live off the fat o' the land. The clergy dinnae help; the heid yins are in thrall tae the rich an' there's no' much Christian charity. But onybody can see there's changes coming. Pamphlets circulating, talk in the coffee hooses, students reading Voltaire and Rousseau. Something's gonnae change soon, sooner than here, at any rate," he added with a smile.

"An' French lassies," said David, nudging Rab. "Tom doesnae say much aboot them at hame, but he'll maybe tell you."

"There's no' much tae tell," said Tom. "I thocht I was in love, I lost her an' noo I'm back hame wi' a bad reputation."

Mungo snorted gleefully.

"Ye hae my sympathy," said Rab. "But dae ye no' hanker after gaun' back? I would."

"Maybe one day," said Tom, thinking of the smugglers and wondering if he and Mungo would soon be stowing away on a ship for France or enlisting in the army to get away. He shuddered and changed the subject.

"Ye farm wi' ye faither, David says."

Rab's face darkened. "Aye, my faither an' my brither Gilbert. It's a hard life. Faither's no keepin' well, he's worn oot. We dae oor best, but I fear this weather'll finish him an' we havenae got the money tae improve the farm."

"An' yersel?" asked Tom, sensing a deep melancholy streak in Rab.

"I want tae get awa'. I tried flax-dressing in Irvine last year but it's as bad as farming, maybe worse. I've educated mysel', I'm curious aboot the world. There must be somethin' mair in life forbye thankless drudgery."

Mungo stood up abruptly. "I'll get the next roon' in," he said and stomped off to speak to the landlord.

"Wha stole his scone?" asked David.

"Hard tae say," replied Tom. "He's aye like that. His mood changes faster than the weather, even the weather here. Ye get used tae it."

Sure enough, when Mungo came back he was all smiles. "I've ordered some whisky wi' the ale. My shout. Mr Cunningham's gi'en me a bonus, he's that pleased wi' my work." He turned to Rab. "Ye've an eye for the lassies yersel', I hear," he said with a leer.

Rab's expressive face darkened. "That's my business," he said shortly, and turned the talk back to farming. He was anxious to hear about the changes David was making at Barnessie; he was changing gradually from rigs to enclosed fields, and had just bought a new iron plough.

"Aye, it's an easier life for them that can afford it," said Rab. "I'd even enjoy the work if it wasnae sae hard."

"Steam power," said Tom. "That's the future," and as the others looked at him, puzzled, he went on, "Aye, if we harnessed the power o' steam, we could cut doon a lot o' the drudgery."

"Listen tae my wee brither," jeered David. "Ye'd think he kent somethin' aboot farmin', him that never gets his haunds dirty."

"No, listen," said Tom. "When I was in Paris I saw this contraption at the Arsenal. It was a like a big cart wi' a great muckle boiler on the front, that produced steam tae drive the wheels. A *fardier,* they cried it, an' Cugnot, the man that built it, had it moving."

"Naw," said Mungo, "Ye're haein' us on."

"It's true," protested Tom, "I've seen it wi' my ain een."

"But did ye see it move?" asked Rab.

Tom had to confess he hadn't.

"It kept bumpin' intae things, they say, so they've parked it in a yard oot o' the way. But you mark my words, in a hundred years or so they'll no need horses tae pull carts an' carriages, it'll a' be done by steam."

"Aye, an' naebody'll need tae work," said Mungo bitterly. "We'll a' live in fine hooses, wear silk an' dine on roast beef an' fine wine. Pigs'll fly an' a'." He stood up abruptly.

"I'm off hame noo. I need tae see tae my mither."

Tom looked up in surprise. Mungo didn't usually show such concern. "Will I come wi' ye?" he asked, remembering Mungo's fear of being in the streets alone.

"Dinnae bother," said Mungo. "I'm a big boy. I'll be fine." But Rab declared that he had to get back to Lochlie and offered to see Mungo round to Mill Street. "I'd like tae hear mair aboot the wine trade," he said to Mungo with a smile. Tom was surprised and pleased to see Mungo smile back; Rab obviously had charm. They said their goodbyes, leaving the brothers alone.

"One for the road?" asked David.

"I'll get them," said Tom. When he came back with two reaming tankards David said, "What dae ye think o' Rab?"

"I like him fine. He's got somethin' aboot him, an' it's no' just his claes."

"Aye, I ken what ye mean. He's a bit o' a dandy. What colour would ye say yon plaid o' his was?"

"I dinnae ken. I've never seen ocht like it, no' even in Paris. It must hae come frae Fleming's."

They drank companionably for a few minutes, then David said, "He's a queer fish, yon Mungo."

"He's worried."

"Aye, there's somethin' on his mind, ye can tell. Dae ye ken what it is?"

Tom thought quickly. The past few days had been difficult. His own worries about the smugglers, Wednesday's adventure and Mungo's constant state of near panic had taken their toll. Before he could change his mind, he found himself confiding in David, telling him about their adventures of the past week.

"So that's whaur ye were last Friday night," said his brother. "I heard ye come in, but I thocht ye'd been wi' a lassie." Tom smiled ruefully. "And that's nane o' my business. But Wednesday – I saw ye come in but I just thocht ye'd got caught in a downpour. I'd nae idea ye were near drowned."

"It was worse for Mungo. He cannae swim." Tom smiled at the memory.

"What aboot Mr Cunningham? Is he mixed up in the smuggling?"

"I dinnae think so, but I cannae be sure. He's gey friendly wi' Adam Kennedy these days."

"Why dae ye no' ask him? If he is in on it, ye'll need tae get awa' frae here quick."

"An' if he's no'?"

"If he's no', an' he finds oot ye kent aboot it and didnae tell him, it's nearly as bad."

Tom saw the wisdom of this; it was what he hadn't dared admit to himself ever since he had first suspected there was smuggling going on.

"Anyway," said David, "ye'll dae as ye think best. Let's get hame noo."

"You go," said Tom, making up his mind. "I'll gang and see if Mr Cunningham's still in the office. It's best tae be clear aboot it."

But when his brother left he began to have doubts. He sat for a while brooding over another tankard of ale, but eventually reached a decision. He stood up, wrapped his plaid around his shoulders and set off down the High Street towards the bridge.

It was dark by now, and drizzling with rain. There were few souls about, few lights in the windows and Tom groped his way through the mirk, slithering on the wet cobbles of the bridge. A cold wind was blowing in from the Firth, tugging at his clothes as he entered Cunningham's yard. There was a single lamp still burning in his employer's window. Tom swallowed nervously, told himself to be brave and set off up the wet stairs.

The outer office door was open. He entered and crossed the room quickly before he could change his mind. He knocked gently on the inner door. There was no reply. He knocked again, a little more loudly. Still nothing.

"He must hae fallen asleep," thought Tom. Tentatively, he tried the door. It was unlocked, and swung open at his touch.

"Mr Cunningham," he began as he stepped inside, then gasped in horror at the sight which met his eyes. Behind his desk, Richard Cunningham lay slumped back in his chair, his eyes staring in shocked surprise, but there was no light in them, any more. There were three great wounds in his chest, still bleeding profusely, and blood everywhere; more, it seemed, than one body could contain.

Tom, stricken numb with shock and horror, had barely time to register the scene before footsteps pounded up the stairs and he was roughly shouldered out of the way. A great cry went up and turning, Tom saw the black-clad skeletal figure of James Cunningham.

"What means this?" he roared.

"Mr Cunningham, I . . ."

James Cunningham stepped closer and in the flickering lamplight Tom saw him gaze at the mangled body of his brother, his face contorted by grief and rage. He composed himself with difficulty, turned back to Tom and said, coldly furious, "Ye'll hang for this, laddie."

For a few seconds the two men stared at each other, then Tom, seized by blind panic, turned and stumbled down the stairs, across the yard and out on to the quayside, pursued by Cunningham. His heart was pounding and his legs could hardly carry him, but at least Cunningham wasn't gaining on him.

As he slipped and stumbled along the quay, he heard the approach of tramping feet and saw the flare of torches up ahead.

"Watchmen!" cried Cunningham behind him. "Ower here!"

Tom, caught between the two, could do nothing. Rough hands seized him, a flaming torch was held close to his face and a tall, broad-shouldered man peered at him.

"What's going on here?" he demanded.

James Cunningham, panting, told how he had found Tom standing over the body of his brother. "This young devil murdered my brither!" he cried. "He should hang, now!"

Tom tried in vain to protest. "I found him. He was already deid," but his words sounded hollow, even to him.

The captain of the watch went into the yard and after climbing the stairs to see the grisly scene for himself, came back, shaking his head sorrowfully. "He's still warm; no lang deid. We'll need tae tak ye in tae the Tolbooth, laddie."

There was nothing to be done. Tom was surrounded by the hefty men of the watch and led away. As he passed Cunningham, he risked a glance at him and in the flaring torchlight thought he caught a glimpse of something that wasn't grief in the deep, dark eyes.

The procession, with Tom in its midst, retraced the route he had taken only a short time earlier, but his thoughts were in such a whirl that he barely noticed the cold night mist as he stumbled over the slippery cobblestones. He shivered at the thought of the Tolbooth. Everyone in Ayr knew it but no-one went willingly into that grim place.

All too soon they arrived beneath the tall forbidding walls. The Tolbooth stood near the river in the centre of the town, an implacable reminder to the citizens of the punishment meted out to wrongdoers. The captain of the watch raised his staff and knocked loudly on the door. Nothing happened for a while but eventually they heard a bolt being drawn back and the face of an ancient gaoler appeared framed in a small window.

"What's yer business?" he grumbled.

"Ye've tae tak' this lad intae custody."

The gaoler wheezed and grumbled some more before the heavy door swung open and Tom and his captors were ushered inside. The old man set his candle on a rough deal table in the entrance and looked Tom up and down.

"Ye're a fine, fancy laddie an' nae mistake," he pronounced. "Name?"

Tom, struck dumb with fear, eventually managed, "Thomas Boyd."

"What's the charge?" asked the gaoler, turning to the watchmen.

"Murder. It's Richard Cunningham, the merchant. His brither found this yin standin' ower the corpse."

"Weel, weel." The gaoler shook his head, eyed Tom up and

down again, then opened a large ledger, took up a quill and began to enter the details.

"Whaur dae ye bide, lad? Wha's yer kin?"

Tom hesitated. He was reluctant to name his family, but they would find out soon enough. He was overcome with fear and shame.

"I ... I ... live at Barnessie House," he stammered. "My faither is Sir Malcolm Boyd," he went on, aiming for a firm voice but ending on a squeak.

There was a stunned silence. The gaoler stared at Tom for what seemed like minutes, then scratched his head sadly.

"Weel, weel. I doubt yer faither can save ye frae what's comin' tae ye."

Shaking his head, he took down a large bunch of keys from a nail in the wall, selected one and said, "Come wi' me." Holding his candle aloft he led Tom, flanked by two stout watchmen with the captain bringing up the rear, through a maze of gloomy corridors. Arriving at a low door, he stood aside for Tom to enter, then slammed the door shut and turned the key. He and the watchmen disappeared, taking the candle with them.

Left alone in utter darkness, Tom groped his way around the wet, slimy walls, cursing as he tripped over a bucket. The stench told him what it was used for; also that it had not been emptied for a while. Trying to keep his feet clear of the stinking mess he felt his way to a rough plank which hung from chains about three feet from the floor and sat down warily.

He tried to work out where he was. There was no light at all and the air was heavy and clammy, so he guessed he was somewhere in the bowels of the building. Gradually he became aware of sounds; a scampering and squeaking which suggested rats – he fancied he could see red eyes glowing at him out of the darkness – then a low moaning from a nearby cell.

Suddenly, someone cried out in anguish, "Mother!" then all was silent. Moments later, the moaning and groaning started again and continued as Tom stretched out gingerly on the hard plank and tried to control the tumult of his thoughts. His mind was full of pictures of horror; he saw again the twisted body of Richard Cunningham, the gaping wounds, the blood. He wondered if these images would remain with him forever. He could not even make sense of his situation at first, so great was his horror.

After the horror came abject fear, which made Tom tremble from head to foot. He was accused of murder! He would be tried and condemned, his family would never recover from the shame, he would hang ... at this thought, every vestige of self-control fled and he began to sob miserably, great racking sobs which shook his whole being. At length, there was a loud banging on the door of his cell and a voice, he thought it was the gaoler, shouted, "Haud yer wheesht, will ye? There's many worse off than you."

Gradually, as weariness overtook him, Tom calmed down and tried to sleep, but when he closed his eyes the images of horror started up again and it was not until well into the morning, when some glimmers of daylight in the dim corridor allowed him to gauge the contours of his cell, that he fell at last into a heavy sleep.

CHAPTER 15

Saturday September 1st

The breeze from the sea lifted the skirts of the women and stirred the ribbons on their caps as the crowd on the Borough Muir gathered for the hanging. There was an almost holiday atmosphere as folk called cheerful greetings to friends and neighbours and hoisted children on their shoulders to get a better view of the edifying spectacle of justice being done. The smell of twopenny ale mingled with that of unwashed clothes and the meaty odour of mutton pies.

The crowd was exceptionally large as the condemned man, a member of one of Ayr's leading families, had been found guilty of a particularly heinous murder which had profoundly shocked the whole community. Bets were laid: would he make a good end or would he have to be dragged screaming to the gallows?

Tom stood on the raised platform beside the ladder which in a few moments he would have to climb to be launched into eternity. He could see the stern face of his father, the steadfast gaze of his brother, wishing him courage, and the weeping figures of his mother and Alison, clinging together for support. Further off stood Bob and Jeanie – he hoped Jeanie's pies had sold well – and Mrs Cunningham, draped in black widow's weeds, supported by Adam Kennedy. Lastly, he spied the gloomy figure of James Cunningham, wearing an expression of grim satisfaction.

Tom felt curiously detached from proceedings – what was life, after all? Feeling the hangman's hand on his shoulder, he turned towards the ladder ...

"Thomas, Thomas," cried a voice and rough hands shook him by the shoulder. Tom awoke with a start, blinking in the light of a candle held close to his face. Relief that he had only been dreaming was swiftly followed by despair as reality came flooding back and he recognised his father's voice.

"Get up, Tom, we're going hame."

The remnants of his dream still clung to Tom's consciousness as, dazed, he stumbled after his father through the open cell door and along the grim passageway, past the grinning old gaoler. "Ye'll be back soon, laddie," he called as father and son went out into the bustling street where Bob waited with the family coach.

"How...?" he asked his father as soon as they were under way.

"Dinnae speir ower much, my lad. Let's just say these lodges are handy, whiles. I went tae the sheriff as soon as I heard and he's released ye intae my custody, for a week."

"A week?"

"Aye, nae mair, an' ye're no' tae leave hame nor gang oot without a member o' the household wi' ye."

"What guid can that dae? They may as weel hang me noo and be finished wi' it."

Tom's voice rose on a note of despair and he clutched at his neck, where he fancied he felt the noose tighten.

"Wheesht, noo, son," said Sir Malcolm. "We'll talk when ye've eaten."

*

That afternoon there was a family conference at Barnessie House. Ranged round the table were Sir Malcolm and Lady Margaret, David, Tom, Bob and Alison Fleming, who had come earlier to discuss Lady Margaret's new gown and who had stayed to eat with the family. Tom had asked that she be allowed to take part in their discussion and his parents, who were impressed by Alison's calm wisdom, had readily agreed.

Under skilful questioning by his lawyer father Tom told his tale in detail, including the smuggling and ending with the discovery of Richard Cunningham's body and his subsequent arrest. The others listened in silence. When he had finished, Sir Malcolm added, "As I tellt the sheriff, my son's maybe a gormless young gowk but he's nae murderer. I think he was inclined tae agree, for he's gi'en us a week tae try and find the culprit."

"Is that no' the sheriff's job?" asked David.

"Aye, but he disnae ken the folk involved, nor the circumstances an' he'd be glad o' oor help, even if we're biased towards Tom. He says he'll be the judge o' what we find, an' if we're nae further forward by next Saturday, Tom will be back in gaol. It maybe disnae seem like it, but it's a big favour he's daein' us."

"But we've nae mair idea than the sheriff wha the culprit is," said Tom.

"That's why we're having this discussion," said his sire patiently. "We need tae consider *cui bono?* – who stands tae profit from Richard Cunningham's death."

"Kennedy and the smugglers," said David promptly. "They'd ken Mr Cunningham was working late and that the office was open. Forbye, it's weel kent Adam Kennedy's a ruthless man."

"But why noo?" asked Tom. "The smuggling seems tae have gone on for years and Mr Cunningham might even have been in on it. That's why I went tae see him; tae be clear aboot it."

"We'll never ken noo if he was in on it or no'," said his father. "We'll say the Kennedy crew had the means and the opportunity and probably a motive, even if it's no' a very strong one."

Tom suddenly remembered Richard Cunningham's words as he left the previous evening.

"Mr Cunningham said he was staying late because there was something in the accounts that didnae add up."

"So it could be to do wi' the smuggling," said Sir Malcolm, "but I reckon he must hae suspected long since that it went on and turned a blind eye, either because it suited him or because they were threatening him. If Kennedy did it, we need tae find oot what had changed that made him turn tae murder."

"I've just remembered something else," said Tom. "When we were leaving, he said his wife was coming by later on."

"Did he noo?" said his father softly. "What time was that?"

"Mungo an' me, we left at six, an' when I went back it was near ten o'clock."

"So she could hae gone there and left again. We'd need tae ask her if she saw anything," said Lady Margaret.

Her husband hesitated, then said, "Unless she did it."

There were gasps of shock around the table. The idea seemed monstrous. Tom tried to picture fastidious, elegant Isabelle Cunningham wielding a knife but his imagination baulked at the idea.

"Nevertheless, we have tae consider every possibility," said Sir Malcolm. "Tom. I ken it's hard for ye, but could ye describe what the body looked like?"

Tom hesitated. "There's ladies here," he muttered.

His mother and Alison hastily assured him that he need have no qualms on their account, and Tom described the position of the body and the wounds, leaving out the part which preyed most on his mind, the blood.

"This then was no cold-blooded murder," opined Sir Malcolm. "It was a frenzied attack by someone in a towering rage. We cannae rule out a *crime passionnel*."

"But would Mrs Cunningham hae the strength tae dae it?" asked Davie.

Tom remembered helping Isabelle dismount the day of her previous visit to the offices and the surprisingly strong grip of her hands. Yes, she probably was physically capable of the crime.

"A woman in a rage can be gey strang," said his father, with a glance at his wife. "Ye mind thon time I forgot tae tak my boots off and got glaur a' ower the new carpet. Ye fairly dinged me then."

Lady Margaret cleared her throat but said nothing. Alison and she exchanged a sympathetic glance.

"If they'd quarrelled aboot something she could hae done it," said David. "Wha kens the secrets o' a marriage?"

"Wha indeed," said his father. There was a moment's lull

before he went on, "The sheriff tells me they havenae found the weapon. He reckons it was a knife, quite wee but very sharp, used wi' a lot o' force."

Again there was silence as they tried to picture Isabelle Cunningham with a small sharp knife. Tom still couldn't manage it.

"Wha else?" asked Sir Malcolm eventually.

"Well, there's Mungo," said David. "He kent the offices better nor onybody."

"But he was wi' us in The Plough yestreen," protested Tom.

"Aye, but he left wi' Rab, a while afore us. He could hae gone back tae the yard."

"I cannae see him daein' it. He moans aboot the work an' aboot everybody in the yard, but he's aye spoken wi' great respect aboot Mr Cunningham."

"But he was acting queer yesterday. Ye mind I said that."

"He's scared oot o' his wits," said Tom. "Ever since Kennedy saw us at Culzean he's in mortal fear a' the time." *Like me*, he thought, then told himself to pull himself together. His family were trying to help, but he didn't think there was much they could do. He felt the constriction round his throat again.

"We'll need tae include him," said Sir Malcolm. "At least till we've had a chance tae talk tae him. Onybody else?"

Bob spoke up for the first time.

"Maybe it wasnae onybody that kent Mr Cunningham weel. Yon's a gey grim neighbourhood doon by the docks. It could hae been ony skellum that saw a licht an' thocht there was gowd tae be had. Ye say yersel' Tam, there's a' sorts in an' oot o' the warehoose cellars at nicht."

"It's possible," said Sir Malcolm, "but if it was, oor chances o' ever findin' them arenae great."

There was a pause while they considered the implications of this for Tom. Finally Alison, who had said nothing until then, spoke up hesitantly. "There's one other person."

"What's that?" cried Sir Malcolm. "Speak up, lass."

Alison looked round the table, her gaze finally resting on Tom.

"Ye said Mr Cunningham's brither had ye arrested."

"Aye, but ..."

"What was he daein' there?"

"Weel, he ...." Tom stopped. "Ye're right. I've never seen him at the warehouse before. He disnae approve o' his brither's trade in the demon drink."

"But he could easily hae wanted tae see Richard on private business," said Lady Margaret. "What kind o' man would kill his ain brither? An' forbye, he's a God-fearing elder o' the kirk."

"Well ...," began Tom, then hesitated, with a look at Alison.

"It's all right, I'll tell them," said she reluctantly, and related her Sabbath encounter with James Cunningham and her meeting with Bessie Gibney. The others listened in mounting shock.

"My puir lass," said Lady Margaret simply.

"I've lang suspected yon man was a hypocrite," said Sir Malcolm, "but tae kill his ain brither. Wha would dae sic a thing?"

"It happens, I fear," said his wife. "Cain and Abel, and mony since."

"Maybe Richard had found oot aboot his activities and threatened tae tak it tae the Session," said David. "It would hae been the end o' him in Ayr."

"So he had a possible motive and certainly the opportunity," said Sir Malcolm. "He could hae done it afore Tom arrived and come back – very fortuitously – when he saw Tom; a handy culprit for him."

There was a pause while those around the table considered the various possibilities. Tom found it hard to believe that any of those mentioned would have killed Richard Cunningham, but somebody had.

Finally, Sir Malcolm summed up. "We hae five groups of suspects – Isabelle Cunningham, James Cunningham, Mungo,

Kennedy and the smugglers, and person or persons unknown. Noo, we'll need a plan o' action. We've only got a week."

As if I could forget, thought Tom.

Various options were discussed, and it was agreed that Bob would visit the dockside taverns and question the drinkers there, David would ask Rab Burns about Mungo's movements and Alison would attend the kirk the next day and try to talk to James Cunningham. This last was objected to vehemently by Tom.

"Ye cannae dae that; after what he did tae you."

"Dinna worry; I'll mak' sure I'm no left alane wi' him," said Alison. "If I show due repentance for standing up tae him he'll maybe talk tae me."

"Just be careful, lass," said Sir Malcolm.

"I'll be wi' my faither. Cunningham'll no dare molest me if he's there."

"What aboot Mrs Cunningham an' Kennedy?" asked David.

"Maybe a social invitation?" said Lady Margaret. "I could invite Mrs Cunningham for tea – oh," she stopped, seeing the expression on the faces around the table, "yes, I see. If she thinks my son killed her husband, she's no likely tae accept . . ." her voice tailed off in embarrassment.

"Maybe I could help there," said Alison. "I've had some orders frae her that I've finished and she's been pleased. I think I could ca' on her."

"Ye're daein' a lot for us," said Sir Malcolm.

"I dinnae like tae see injustice, an' forbye, I'm no part o' your family, so it's easier for me."

"Weel, if ye can find oot onything, we'll a' be in your debt."

They agreed that it would be difficult, if not impossible, to inquire into the actions of Kennedy and the other smugglers. None of them could enter the warehouse openly and indeed, it was uncertain what the future of Richard Cunningham's business would be.

Tom, who had been silent for a while, asked, "What aboot

me? What can I dae? I cannae just sit around waitin' for them tae come for me."

"The sheriff says ye're aye tae hae a member o' the family wi' ye an' ye're no' tae leave hame," said his father. "Forbye, I doot ye'd want tae show yer face in the toon; it's ower dangerous."

There was little more to be said, so Lady Margaret rang for tea. When Jeanie appeared, she brought a message.

"There's a laddie doon in the kitchen speirin' efter Master Tom. Red hair, plooks, mouthy.."

"That'll be Mungo," said Tom. "Maybe he has some news."

He found Mungo in the stable-yard, absently kicking at one of the hitching posts. His gloomy expression brightened a little when he saw Tom.

"Tom, thank the Lord ye're here an' no in gaol. What's gaun on, man? I went tae work this forenoon an' it's a' tapsalteerie at the yard. They said Mr Cunningham's deid an' you were in the Tolbooth. I went there but they said ye'd gone. What's happenin'?"

"Did ye come a' this way on foot?"

"Aye, I've been wanderin' aboot for a while. What's gaun on?" he asked again.

Tom explained about finding Mr Cunningham's body, his arrest and his father's intervention.

"What are they sayin' at the warehoose?" he asked.

"They'll no talk tae me. Kennedy has closed up the yard an' he said he'd slit my throat for me if I showed up there again. What am I gonnae dae, Tom? He looked murderous. I'm in mortal fear, I tell ye, man."

"It's me they suspect," said Tom. "Surely they'll leave you alone, noo."

"There's still the smuggling. I ken ower much aboot that. They'll kill me an' dump me in the river if I gang back there again. Please, Tom, can I bide here for a bit?"

Tom hesitated. He could see that Mungo was in an even greater state of terror than before, but on the other hand, he was a suspect. But again, perhaps it was better to have him here, where they could watch and perhaps question him.

"Ye're no feart I'm the murderer?" he asked.

"Naw," said Mungo at once. "Ye'd nae reason tae kill him and ye havenae got it in ye; onybody can see that."

"Somebody killed him, though."

Both were silent, thinking back to the last time they had seen Richard Cunningham, less than a day before.

"He was a guid man," said Tom. "He didnae deserve sic an end."

"No," agreed Mungo quietly.

At that moment Lady Margaret emerged from the house with Alison, who was taking her leave. Both women paused on seeing Mungo. Tom hastily introduced him and Mungo bowed awkwardly to his mother as Alison, whose first sight of the mysterious Mungo this was, looked on inquisitively.

"Have ye come a' this way on foot, Mr McGillivray?" asked Lady Margaret. "Ye must be weary. Come awa' in. We're just having tea. Ye must join us. Thank you for coming, Mistress Fleming," she added, turning to Alison, "and for a' ye've done. I'll leave ye wi' Tom," and with a smile, she took Mungo's arm and led him towards the house.

"She's a marvel, your mother," said Alison. "She never forgets the social graces."

"Aye, she'd be servin' tea in an earthquake," said Tom, with a fond smile at his parent's retreating back.

"So that's Mungo. I've aye wondered what he was like."

"He's no sae bad, an' he's scared stiff. He cannae gang back tae Cunningham's noo, either. He was askin' if he could stay here."

"Would ye want that?"

"It might be safer for him, an' we could keep an eye on him here."

"I suppose that's true. I still think he should take care o' his ain mither." Alison gave a rueful smile; she knew she and Tom would never agree on that score. "I'd better awa'," she added. "Faither will be worried." She crossed the yard to where her donkey was placidly chewing a tuft of grass, untethered her and mounted.

"When will I see ye again?" asked Tom, feeling suddenly bereft.

"I'll gang tae the kirk the morn, an' see what I can find oot, an' maybe call here in the evening."

"Tak' care, then," said Tom, with a long look into her face.

Alison coloured. "I will. Fare thee weel, Tom."

She dug her heels into Jinty's flanks and donkey and girl trotted off in the direction of Ayr. She did not look back.

*

Upstairs, Tom found Mungo ensconced on the brocade sofa in the sitting room, balancing a plate of scones on his knee, blushing furiously as Lady Margaret refilled his teacup.

"Ah, Tom," she said, "Mr McGillivray has been telling me aboot his situation. I think it would be best if he could bide here for a while. Ayr is a dangerous place for him, from what I gather."

For some reason, the idea did not please Tom, although he could not think why. Probably because if this was to be his last ever week with his family, he did not want a stranger in their midst. He told himself firmly not to be so uncharitable.

"What aboot your mither?" he asked.

"Och, she's used tae seein' tae hersel'," said Mungo blithely. "Forbye, she's been lookin' a bit better lately, drinkin' less."

"We can send a message tae her, if ye like," said Lady Margaret.

"Dinnae bother, ma'am. She kens I'll likely be here. Could I hae another o' yer delicious scones?"

*

The rest of the day passed off without incident. In the evening, when he judged that his son's mood was conducive to it, Sir Malcolm questioned Tom at length about the exact circumstances of the crime. "If ye tell me a' ye can, afore ye forget, there's maybe a wee detail that disnae seem important but could be usefu' later."

Tom patiently told all he could remember, several times over, but the pain of the telling did not lessen.

"Did ye see a weapon?" asked his father suddenly.

Tom pictured the scene once more – the body slumped in the chair, the gaping wounds, the blood . . .

"No," he said finally. "It must hae been a knife, but there wasnae one there. At least, nane that I could see."

"Onything oot o' place?"

"No. It's aye tidy in Mr Cunningham's office."

"What was on the desk?"

"Just an inkwell an' some quills and oh aye, there was a book open on the blotter."

"What kind o' book?"

"A big ledger; an account book, I think. Mr Cunningham had been working late gaun ower the accounts for the past few months. He does . . . did this twice a year."

"Could ye smell onything?"

Tom thought back. He closed his eyes and pictured the scene.

"Blood," he sighed. "It smelled like a butcher's shop." He shuddered. "Yon rusty smell. Tobacco – Mr Cunningham smokes a pipe whiles." He hesitated.

"Ocht else?" prompted his father.

"Perfume," he said slowly as the memory came back. A faint, elusive scent. Into his mind came a memory of mocking dark eyes and shapely hands on his arms as helped the lady dismount.

"I think it was Mrs Cunningham's. It was quite faint, but I'm sure the scent was there."

"So Mrs Cunningham probably did gang tae the offices at some point in the evening. Weel remembered, Tom. Noo, yer friend Mungo. What dae ye make o' him?"

"Weel, he's a queer fish a' right. Alison says he treats his mither shamefully, but he says Annie was aye a hopeless drunk, half oot o' her mind, best left tae hersel'. Says he's tried tae help her but there's naethin' tae be done. He has tae work, so o' course she's left on her ain."

"Dae ye think he could hae killed Richard Cunningham?"

Tom hesitated. Finally he said, "It's possible but I dinnae think sae. His moods shift like the tides, an' his imagination runs away wi' him, but he's aye been loyal tae Mr Cunningham. He kens his livelihood depends on him an' forbye, he seems genuinely fond o' him. Mungo's aye feart o' something – he's in a panic because he thinks Adam Kennedy's oot tae kill us."

"An' you're no? In a panic?"

"That or the hangman," said Tom ruefully. "However ye look at it, I'd say my prospects were dim."

He sounded calm, but was aware of mounting despair within him. "Can we stop noo, faither?"

"Aye, son." Sir Malcolm sighed. They were not much further forward. "If ye think o' onything else, mind ye tell me richt awa."

As his son left the room, Sir Malcolm heaved a great sigh. He had to remain practical for Tom's sake, but he could see no way out, either.

*

Feeling the need for exercise, Tom went out in the gloaming to take a turn round the gardens. As he passed the walled orchard he was surprised to hear voices from within and more surprised to see Katie, in her favourite seat on the swing, engaged in earnest conversation with Mungo, who sat crouched in the damp grass. His young sister had been excluded from the family discussion earlier but had learned what she could from Jeanie and Bob and was now quizzing Mungo. Tom had been about to interrupt them but some instinct made him draw back behind the wall to listen.

"It must be interesting tae work for a wine importer," Kate

was saying, copying her mother's best "social graces" manner. "Do tell me mair."

Involuntarily, Tom smiled. He could picture Mungo torn between his desire to tell the child to mind her own business and his natural boastfulness. Boastfulness won.

"Well, I've been chief clerk – accountant ye might say, for some years now. The work is very interesting and varied," – Tom smiled again, remembering Mungo's frequent grumbles about the repetitive tasks his job entailed – "and of course I hae considerable responsibility, or I had, until the recent unfortunate turn of events."

Kate wisely chose not to question him further about that at this stage. Instead she said, "And ye work wi' my brither. What's that like?"

"Weel, of course I had tae spend a lot of time showing him the ropes. He's a mite slow on the uptake" – Tom suppressed an indignant splutter – "but I think my hard work and patience hae paid off. He's able tae work independently maist o' the time noo."

Tom, remembering his mother's warnings that eavesdroppers get their just deserts, tried to see the funny side of this.

"And on a personal level?" enquired Kate.

Good grief, thought Tom, *where does she get it from?* Probably from a lot of eavesdropping during their mother's tea parties, he realised. He knew about her favourite spot on the landing by the sitting room door.

"A personal level? We get along fine, maist o' the time. He's a pleasant enough lad, but awfu' vain. I dinnae think spendin' years in Paris was guid for him. He thinks he's the bees' knees, swannin' aboot in his fancy blue coat."

Tom had heard enough. He gave a warning cough, then stepped through the gate in the wall. If he had hoped to surprise them, he was mistaken.

"Ah Tom," said Kate. "We were just talkin' aboot ye."

"I heard," muttered Tom.

Mungo burst out laughing.

"The look on yer face, ye daft gowk. We heard ye comin.'"

"We kent fine ye were there," added Kate. "It was just a bit o' fun."

Tom grinned through gritted teeth. He wasn't sure Mungo had been joking.

"I think supper's ready. Let's go in," he said.

CHAPTER 16

Sunday September 2nd

The rain clouds had moved in again overnight, shrouding the narrow streets in Sabbath gloom. Alison and her father set off for the kirk in a persistent, soaking drizzle. The lowering grey skies matched the sombre mood of the congregation as they gathered to remember Richard Cunningham, so cruelly snatched from their midst in the prime of life.

The Boyd family pew was nearly empty. Lady Margaret had wanted to attend, but Sir Malcolm had decreed that it was better to stay away. The only occupants were the Misses McFadzean, sombre for once in dress and demeanour, and Alison blessed them silently for their decision to represent the family. Looking around, she noticed that Isabelle Cunningham was also absent.

After the opening hymn and the Lord's Prayer came the Old Testament reading. Alison started when she saw James Cunningham rise and make his way to the lectern. He opened the Bible and looked round at the curious faces of the congregation.

"The reading," he said, "is from Deuteronomy chapter 32." He cleared his throat, and his harsh voice thundered, *"To me belongeth vengeance, and recompense; their foot shall slide in due time: for the day of their calamity is at hand, and the things that shall come upon them make haste."* His black eyes glittered in his gaunt white face as he stared at the Boyd pew, where the Misses McFadzean sat. A frisson of fear went round the congregation and Miss Letty McFadzean let out a low groan while her sister trembled uncontrollably. Alison noticed however that they did not drop their eyes before the elder's venomous stare.

The minister's sermon, likewise on the theme of vengeance, did nothing to alleviate the gloom and Alison was relieved when the service was over and they could leave the church.

The rain had let up and a pale watery sun was trying to penetrate the clouds. Alison, shivering in her thin shawl, would have dearly loved to go straight home, but aware of her promise to Tom's family she clutched her father's arm and joined the line of people waiting to offer words of sympathy to James Cunningham. As the line shuffled nearer she began to tremble, remembering her last encounter with the man.

When it was their turn she braced herself and held out her hand. She could not look into those hooded black eyes but with as much dignity as she could muster she mumbled, "I'm truly sorry, sir. Please accept my condolences."

There was a moment's silence, an eternity to Alison. Cunningham ignored her outstretched hand, said loudly "I've nothing tae say tae ye, mistress," and turned pointedly to the next well-wishers. The exchange was not lost on the congregation. There were a few hisses of indrawn breath and somewhere, someone sniggered. Alison was momentarily at a loss, conscious of inquisitive eyes on her, but she straightened her shoulders, took her father's arm again and they moved off towards the yett, followed by many a curious stare.

*

"Thank you, ma'am." Alison smiled gratefully as she accepted a cup of tea from Lady Margaret. The evening was chilly and a fire had been lit in the sitting-room where the family had gathered to hear Alison's report, but the fire, the tea and the warmth of the welcome did nothing to dispel her feeling of gloomy foreboding.

The family listened in silence as she described the scene in the kirk and her encounter with James Cunningham.

"He just ignored me," she said ruefully. "There was nothing I could dae. I felt heart-sorry for your sisters," she added, turning to Lady Margaret. "Tae have thon man's ire directed at them in the Lord's hoose, an' a' the mutterings afterwards, but they didnae flinch."

"Aye, they were brave," said Sir Malcolm. "Mair nor we deserved, maybe."

"Ye were right, though," said his wife. "We couldnae hae gone tae the kirk, in the circumstances. My sisters kent that." But she was glad to hear her husband praise them for once.

"Was Mrs Cunningham no there?" asked Tom.

"No," replied Alison, turning towards him. She hesitated, knowing her other item of news would dismay the family further.

"I ... I did try tae call on her afore I came here," she admitted, "but she wasnae receiving visitors. The servant shut the door in my face. They say she's prostrate wi' grief."

There was a silence. All were reminded that a woman had lost her beloved husband but also that they had drawn two blanks in their investigations.

"I'm truly sorry," said Alison. "I thocht I could help, but it seems I've done mair harm than good."

"Ye've done nae harm, my dear," said Lady Margaret, "and we're grateful tae ye for trying. It couldnae hae been easy."

"No," said Alison, remembering the hatred in James Cunningham's eyes and the stony face of Isabelle's maid, "it wasn't."

"Pity it did nae guid," muttered Tom bitterly.

Another silence. They had all heard.

Tom and Alison stared at each other for a moment, then Alison, red-faced, stood up abruptly.

"I'd better go," she said, and as Lady Margaret rose too, "please, I can find my ain way oot. Thank ye for your hospitality." And with that she hurried from the room, head held high.

"Thomas, how could ye?" cried his mother as Tom too headed for the door. She got no reply. The door banged behind him and they heard his angry steps climbing the stairs to his room on the next floor.

"Lovers' tiff," opined Mungo with a grin. No-one answered.

*

Some time later, when it was already dark, Lady Margaret knocked tentatively on her son's door. There was no reply. She knocked again, a little louder, and called, "Tom, are ye all right?" Eventually she heard a movement and the door was flung open. Tom stood there, but couldn't look her in the eye. Raising her candle, she was shocked by her son's dishevelled appearance and the signs of tears on his face.

"Oh, son." She set the candle down by the bed and reached up to hug him as best she could, then pulled him down beside her on the bed and cradled his head in her lap as she had done when he was a child. He was still only twenty, she reminded herself, not quite a man yet. She stroked his thick black hair as he sobbed out his grief, murmuring soothing words until the crying subsided and he sat up.

"Sorry, mither," he muttered. "I've soaked yer dress."

"It'll dry," she replied. "Dae ye want tae talk?"

Tom heaved a great sigh. "I'd gie onything tae tak' back what I said. Alison did mair tae help nor ony o' us, an' a' I could dae was moan. And noo I've lost her."

"It was rude, Tom, but when Alison thinks aboot it she'll understand ye were disappointed. She kens your situation."

Both were silent, seeing the hangman's noose in their minds. Margaret reached for her son again and they clung together for a few moments. Then, gently freeing herself, she said, "We have tae be strong, and hope and pray for a way out. We still hae time."

"Aye, but if I've lost Alison, they may as weel hang me noo."

"*So he loves her,*" thought Lady Margaret. *"My puir bairn."*

CHAPTER 17

Monday September 3rd

———

The next day brought no change. The rain started early and seemed to have set in forever, the steady drizzle finding its way through layers of garments to chill the wearer to the bone. Tom stood in the orchard, oblivious to the rain, glad to be out of the house but all too aware that his home was his prison now. His father had shut himself in his study just after breakfast, David was in the fields, shaking his head in despair at the corn which would not ripen. His mother's looks of loving concern had begun to weigh on him and he was irritated beyond measure by the playful banter between Mungo and Kate, so he had escaped from the house and come to stand here in the rain. He wondered what Alison was doing. She would be busy at her work; did she spare a thought for him at all, and was it a kind one? *Not much chance of that,* he thought. The minutes dragged by, and he almost wished the end of the week would come, so utterly hopeless did he feel.

"Come on, cheer up," said a voice at his elbow. "It's no' the end o' the world, at least, no' till Saturday."

"Mungo . . ." said Tom wearily.

"Thocht ye might need some company."

Tom groaned inwardly.

"Anyway," continued Mungo blithely, "I'm fair grateful tae yer family for takin' me in. It's a load aff my mind. An' yer wee sister, she's great. Sharp as a tack, an' bonnie wi' it."

Tom bit back an angry reply. He could not begrudge Mungo her friendship – he had few enough friends – but his words had brought home to Tom that his wee sister was growing up, and was at a vulnerable age.

"Nae sign o' Alison the day," went on Mungo.

"Dinnae speir efter her. I doot she'll want tae see me again," said Tom, too forlorn to be angry.

"Och, it's no sae bad. What ye said wasnae that bad, an' she'll understand when she thinks on it. She's kind, an' she'll come roon. The lassies aye dae."

Tom felt a little better.

"Just as long as she does afore Saturday," went on Mungo. "It'll be ower late by then. Whaur are ye gaun, Tom?"

*

As the family gathered for a late supper, David took Tom aside. He'd just come back from Ayr, where he'd met Rab Burns at the livestock market. From him he had learned that on the Friday evening Rab had left Mungo at the end of Mill Street.

"He said it was the back o' eight when he left him, an' he seemed cheerful enough. Said he was gaun tae see his mither was comfortable an' then turn in himsel'. Rab saw nae reason tae doubt him."

"It's true, I cannae see him as a murderer; he's feart o' his ain shadow these days. What's the talk in the toon?"

David sighed. "It's a' aboot you an' Mr Cunningham, I fear. I'll no' repeat it, ye dinnae need that."

"So I'm condemned already?"

"It's just that folks are lookin' for a culprit; they dinnae ken ye like your family does, an' they're ready tae believe onything. Ye ken hoo rumours start."

"They'll be sayin' next I learned fornication in the stews o' Paris, I'm Isabelle Cunningham's secret lover an' I killed Mr Cunningham so I could marry the widow an' tak' ower the business."

David hadn't the heart to tell him that that was exactly the kind of wild rumour he had heard.

"Dinnae be daft. Come on, supper's ready; it'll dae ye guid tae eat an' tak a wee dram."

*

Once the mutton stew and bannocks had been served, David turned to Mungo.

"I hope you're no bored hangin' roon the hoose, Mungo," he said.

"I am, a bit," said Mungo, "but I cannae gang oot while Kennedy's efter me."

"You could help me a bit wi' the farm work. We could aye use another pair o' hands."

"Weel, maybe. Aye, I'd like that fine. What aboot Tom?"

"Tom's welcome an' a', but he's no' that bothered aboot manual work, an' he's a bit haundless forbye," he added, turning to his brother.

Before Tom could reply, Mungo chipped in.

"Aye, Tom's mair o' an intellectual, a friend o' the *philosophes*. Forbye, he'd need tae tak' his coat aff, an' he might need a surgeon for that."

There was good-natured laughter around the table. Tom did his best to join in.

"Dae ye think I could hae some mair stew, ma'am?" asked Mungo. "It's delicious."

"Of course, Mungo," said Lady Margaret warmly. "I'm glad tae see you're settling in wi' us."

CHAPTER 18

Tuesday September 4th

———

The next day, David took advantage of a break in the bad weather to start mending the fences in the biggest cornfield. Mungo volunteered to help and showed an unexpected aptitude for the work and a growing interest in farming so that Davie, somewhat to his surprise, was glad of his company. When Kate brought them cheese, bannocks and ale at midday the three of them enjoyed a happy half-hour of banter and laughter while Tom brooded in his room.

At two o'clock Sir Malcolm, who liked to take daily exercise, had his horse saddled and set off for Ayr. Tom wanted to go with him but his father refused, saying he had business to attend to and besides, it was not safe for Tom to show himself in the town.

"Be reasonable, laddie; I cannae tak' ye wi' me," he said. "There's a new Scots Magazine come. Dae some reading."

Tom tried, but the magazine contained too much gloomy news from the American colonies and the many accounts of murder trials and retribution nearer home echoed all too closely his own situation. He wondered, despairingly, how many other innocent souls had been unjustly executed.

At five o'clock the rain came on again.

*

That evening, Bob Balfour pushed open the door of the Anchor Inn by the docks, pausing to shake the rain from his plaid and let his eyes adjust to the dim, smoky interior. Loud voices, raucous laughter and the sound of fiddle music had drawn him to this tavern, the third he had tried. It was a long time since Bob had been out drinking – Jeanie saw to that – and he was aware that he was an unfamiliar figure to the revellers within. For this he was grateful; even regulars from Ayr were unlikely to connect him to the Boyd family.

He had made discreet enquiries in the first two inns he had tried, hoping to find someone who had business with the Cunninghams, but without success. Most of the drinkers in the dockside taverns were sailors off the ships and while some sailed regularly into Ayr, none showed much interest in the town.

Bob fought his way to the bar, bought a tankard of twopenny ale and looked round for a seat and company. He found an empty stool at the end of a long table where a group of men were loudly discussing the state of the American war.

"Reckon it'll be a' ower by the end o' the year," said one, a thickset youth with straw-coloured hair.

"An' a guid thing tae," said another, who bore a family resemblance to the first. "At least we'll hae nae mair need tae hide frae the sodgers. I dinnae fancy bein' forced intae the army."

"My brither was pressed intae the navy," said a third. "An' since then we've had nae word o' him. The De'il kens whaur he is noo."

"Maybe he'll be hame soon, maybe even in one piece. Wullie, it's your shout," said the first speaker.

"Aye, I'm gaun, I'm gaun. Same again Geordie?"

"Aye, an' a wee dram tae chase it. You an' a', Joe?" he added, turning to the third man, who grunted his assent. Wullie went off to the bar.

"Hoo's business, then?" asked Joe.

"Business?"

"Aye, ye ken . . ." Joe touched the side of his nose.

Geordie glanced round, and noticing Bob at the end of the table, lowered his voice. In spite of the noise in the tavern Bob, straining hard to hear while pretending to devote his attention to his drink and the fiddler, could just make out snatches of the conversation.

"... A' tapsalteerie since the boss died ..."

"... maybe it'll be easier noo he's oot o' the way ..."

"... let me ken if there's ony work ..."

"... Kennedy's mair or less in charge noo ..."

Wullie came back from the bar, bearing a stoup of ale and a small flask of whisky. As he made to refill his companions' tankards, he bent to whisper in his brother's ear. Geordie rose and came round the table to stand over Bob, quickly joined by his brother. The fiddler paused and the laughter died away.

"Bob Balfour, isn't it?" enquired Geordie in a quietly menacing tone.

Bob looked up and swallowed. Not for the first time that night he wished he were back in his stable or better, in his warm bed with Jeanie.

"Wha' wants tae ken?" he asked with a bravado he did not feel.

"Never mind. Ye're Sir Malcolm Boyd's groom, aren't ye?" At the mention of the Boyd name, a murmur of interested speculation went round the bar.

There was no point in denying it. Someone at the bar had obviously recognised him. He nodded. "An' wha would you be?" he asked, though by now he had a good idea he was talking to Tom's former colleagues, the McSkimming brothers.

"That's nae concern o' yours," came the reply. "I'll ask ye tae step ootside wi' us. Private business," he added with a leer for the benefit of the assembled company, who were now taking a keen interest in proceedings. There was a ripple of appreciative laughter.

"I'd rather finish my ale in peace," said Bob, turning away from them and raising his tankard. Before he could drink he felt himself hoisted by the elbows. The ale spilled and the tankard rolled onto the floor.

To a chorus of "That's it, Geordie, gi'e the wee bauchle what he deserves," he was lifted off his feet by the two

McSkimmings, carried through the door and dumped onto the wet cobbles of the quayside.

The rain poured down relentlessly as the fiddle music started up again inside. Bob could hear the steady clinking of the ships' masts and in the dim light from the tavern he saw the jeering faces of the McSkimming brothers above him. Geordie had a knife in his hand.

"What's yer business here?" he demanded.

"Nae business. I was just haein' a drink."

"Weel, noo, it seems tae me that if a guid, God-fearin' laddie is let oot drinkin' by his sonsie, sharp-tongued besom o' a wife," here both brothers chuckled gleefully, "Aye, we've heard aboot your Jeanie. If she lets ye oot, there must be a reason. We'd never seen ye here afore, so we speired wha ye might be. Very interesting, we thocht. Sir Malcolm Boyd's groom. An' it seems tae me ye were takin' a great interest in oor conversation."

"Mair nor in the fiddle music," added his brother.

"So I would ca' that spying, would you no, Wullie?"

"Aye."

"An' ye ken what they dae wi' spies, don't ye Bob?"

Bob did not reply. He was miserably aware of the cold rain seeping through his clothes and the knife in Geordie McSkimming's hand. He looked up to see Geordie nodding solemnly as he ran a finger slowly along the blade of the knife. Within the tavern the noise and laughter were again in full swing.

"Naebody tae see or hear," said Geordie silkily. "A quick knife in the ribs an' we dump ye in the harbour. Wi' a few stanes in yer pocket ye'll just disappear."

Bob closed his eyes. As he waited for the blow, thoughts crowded into his head. Would he be dead before he hit the water or would he drown? He didn't fancy either option. What would happen to the family? He was sure now that Kennedy and the McSkimmings were behind Richard Cunningham's death, but what good would that do young Tom? Most of all, he wished he could see Jeanie one more time. How would she manage the cooking without him?

The seconds stretched out agonisingly as he waited, aware of the sharp wet cobbles digging into his knees and almost welcoming the pain, which meant he was still alive.

At length there came a wicked chuckle. "Aye, it warms my heart tae see a man in fear for his life, but maybe no' this time." Rough hands seized him and hauled him to his feet. He opened his eyes and found himself inches from the pock-marked face and beery breath of Geordie McSkimming.

"See here, Bob," he said. "This is what we're gaun tae dae. Wullie here is fair itching tae see the last o' ye, but fortunately for you I'm the boss here. I'm willing tae forget ye stuck yer lang neb intae what disnae concern ye, but only this time, mind. You're tae gang back tae yon fancy black-haired gowk an' remind him he's got a date wi' the hangman, an' Wullie an' me, we'll be in the front row tae watch him dangle. Eh, Wullie?"

His brother looked disappointed that Bob was going to get away, but chortled with glee at the prospect of Tom Boyd on the end of a rope.

"An' if ye *ever* show yer face doon here again, ye ken what'll happen tae ye," went on Geordie, with a flourish of the knife. "Awa' wi ye noo."

Bob was released from his grasp with a violent shove which sent him sprawling on the ground again. The two brothers looked on mockingly as he struggled to his feet, his heart pounding as he slipped and slid on the greasy cobbles.

"Mind ye dinnae fa' in the water, Bob," jeered the younger McSkimming.

*

Two hours later, Bob was sitting by the range in the kitchen, wrapped in a blanket, sipping a hot toddy and being fussed over by Jeanie. He told himself that if he could just stop shaking he would feel better. He glanced up at Tom, who was pacing back and forward between the big table and the range.

"Ye're sure it was the McSkimmings?" he asked.

"Oh aye. Wullie an' Geordie. They ca'd each ither by name, didnae try tae hide it. An' they mentioned Cunningham's warehoose and Adam Kennedy. I'm just sorry I wasnae able tae find oot mair. What are ye daein', wumman?" he winced as Jeanie pulled the blanket aside and applied a foul-smelling cloth to his left knee.

"Haud yer wheesht, man, it's only a mustard poultice. Yer knee's the size o' a fitba'. Ye'll need tae keep the poultice on the nicht if ye want tae be able tae work the morn."

Bob sighed, but submitted himself to her ministrations.

Tom felt once again that he wasn't being grateful enough.

"Hoo can I thank ye, Bob?" he asked, shamefaced. "Ye've risked your life an' damn near got yersel' killed."

"Weel, I'm still here, thank the Lord," said Bob, "an' I'm pretty sure the smugglers are behind it a'."

"What exactly did they say again?"

"I heard Geordie sayin' 'It'll be easier noo he's oot o' the way' and 'Kennedy's in charge noo.' Then they warned me never tae gang near them again." He thought it best not to transmit the message about the hanging.

"I've got tae dae something," muttered Tom. "I cannae just wait here kicking my heels till Saturday. I need tae gang back tae the warehoose."

"But ye're no tae gang near Ayr," said Jeanie. "If they catch ye they'll no need tae wait till Saturday tae string ye up."

"Jeanie . . ." began Bob.

"No, she's right," said Tom. "I'll just need tae mak' sure they dinnae catch me."

"Dinnae tell us ony mair," said Jeanie, "Then we cannae let on. I dinnae fancy tellin' lies tae yer faither. That's enough talk noo, it's gone midnight. Awa' tae yer bed, Tom, an' let me see tae my man."

CHAPTER 19

Wednesday September 5th

———

Overnight, the rain cleared and the next day dawned bright and fair. Tom, confined again to the house, tried not to be annoyed by Mungo's cheerful whistling as he set off for the fields with David, who was bent on harvesting some potatoes and turnips as they waited hopefully for a spell of dry weather to go on with the haymaking.

Sir Malcolm took pity on his son and invited him along on his morning ride. "Fresh air'll dae ye guid; ye're lookin' a mite peely-wally," he said. "We'll no gang far, we cannae risk ye bein' seen." Tom thought of his plans for later in the day. He was going to betray his father's trust, and hoped fervently he would not bring further shame on the family.

As they entered the stables to saddle up they met Bob, who was limping slightly but otherwise none the worse for his ordeal of the previous evening. "The swellin's gone doon," he confirmed. "Thon mustard poultices fair stink but they did the job."

Father and son set off down back lanes past Alloway and on towards the coast. They stopped on the hill overlooking Dunure and its ruined castle on the cliff. Tom was reminded of the day he'd arrived back from France and stopped on the cliffs near here, only a few short weeks before. So much had happened since he'd first looked out over the waters of the Firth, still and deep today in the sunshine. Away to his left Ailsa Craig stood out bright and clear and he wondered if he'd ever see its granite cliffs again. It didn't seem fair; the brightness of the day was a mocking obscenity to one facing his doom.

Timor mortis conturbat me, he thought. He shivered and

looked across at his father. Sir Malcolm, comfortably astride his horse, was studying the castle ruins closely.

"It's a shame they're just letting it gang tae ruin," he observed. "It was a fine building in its day. Ye ken they entertained Queen Mary there back in the auld days? Ye can still see, yonder, whaur the great ha' was. But aye, it's a sorry sicht noo, an' no safe, I'll wager. Nae wonder they're a' building modern places like Culzean."

"Or like yer ain hoose. Barnessie's no' exactly a keep."

"Aye, that tae. There's nae need for yon tall castles built for defence ony mair. Times hae changed for the better ... in some ways" added his father, thinking of Tom's plight. "Ye ken what happened here?"

"Somethin' aboot roastin' an abbot?" Tom's recollection of old tales told him by Jeanie was rather hazy – there had been so many of them.

"Aye, back in 1570. They tortured the abbot, really the commendator of Crossraguel, doon there in the castle dungeons."

"The way Jeanie telt it, they roasted him on a spit," said Tom. "She used tae tell me tales at bedtime tae help me sleep, but I had bad dreams for weeks efter thon yin."

"Jeanie aye likes the bloodiest version o' the auld tales, but it wasnae quite like that. They just toasted his feet a bit tae mak' him gi'e up his claim tae the commendatorship, an' he survived, though he never walked again. Forbye, he was nae holy man or sacrificial lamb. It was a' aboot a money feud between the Kennedys an' the Stewarts." Sir Malcolm sighed. "Weel, Tom, it's nearly dinner-time. We'd best be heading back."

Somewhat reluctantly, they turned their horses away from the shining waters of the Firth and towards Barnessie.

*

Meanwhile, Alison was tidying the shelves in the back shop, trying to get Tom out of her mind. She had parted with him in anger on Sunday and was now tormented by the thought that she might never see him again. That was more than she could bear. She resolved to swallow her pride and ride out to Barnessie the next day.

Just then she heard the shop door open. "I'll be wi' ye richt awa'" she called. She smoothed her apron and patted her hair before going through to the front.

"Guid day tae ye, mistress," said Bessie Gibney.

"Bessie! I'm pleased tae see ye. Hae ye brocht the washing back?" For Alison had been true to her word and sent business Bessie's way.

"I hae that," said Bessie, indicating a large basket of sheets on the floor by her side, from which rose a sweet smell of herbs.

"Thank ye Bessie. Ye've done a guid job. Noo, what dae I owe ye?"

She paid Bessie, who lingered hesitantly by the counter, nervously plucking at her shawl with rough red hands.

"Can I dae ocht for ye, Bessie?" asked Alison. "Ye look worried."

Bessie hesitated, then, making up her mind, she said, "Ye mind when we talked aboot gaun tae the Kirk Session . . ."

"Aye . . ."

"Aboot my weans' faither . . ."

"Aye . . ." repeated Alison in what she hoped was a non-committal but encouraging tone.

"Weel, I was thinkin' . . ."

"Dae ye want me tae come wi' ye?"

Relief flooded Bessie's face. "Would ye, mistress? Only I'm feart tae gang masel'."

"Of course I'll come. But what made ye change yer mind?"

"Promise ye'll no tell onybody?"

"That depends on what it is . . ." began Alison, but seeing Bessie's expression darken she went on, "but I'm mair or less sure ye can tell me in confidence. Come through tae the back shop and we'll talk aboot what tae dae for the best."

She led the way, settled Bessie by the big table with a glass of ale and sat down opposite her.

"Noo, tell me what's troublin' ye. It'll be just between oorsels."

Bessie took a gulp of ale, swallowed nervously and began.

"I had a visit frae him . . . ye ken wha it is . . ."

"James Cunningham," supplied Alison, as it seemed Bessie could not bring herself to say the name.

"Aye, him. He's never affectionate wi' me, I dinnae expect that, but this time, though he was civil enough he frightened me. I'd never seen him like that afore."

"What did he dae?" asked Alison apprehensively, the memory of her own encounter with James Cunningham in that very room fresh in her mind.

"Dae? He didnae dae ocht. Just informed me, cold as ice, that I would get nae mair money oot o' him for my brats. As if it was a' my fault, when it was him that forced me," cried Bessie, beginning to sob.

Alison waited quietly while the girl groped for her apron and scrubbed furiously at her face and eyes. Gradually the sobs subsided, she wiped her face once last time and managed a watery smile.

"What wi' that and a' the business I've lost through standin' in the kirk for my *sins*," – she fairly spat the word out – "I'll soon hae nothin' left. I dinnae care what happens tae me," she added bitterly, "but there's my weans an' my sister. I cannae let them starve. So if ye'd help me, I'll gang tae the session an' tell them what a cold-blooded snake they hae in their midst."

Alison stood up.

"We'll gang directly tae the minister, for Cunningham'll hae cronies on the session. We'd maybe no' get a fair hearing."

"What . . . noo?" asked Bessie, beginning to tremble.

"Richt awa'," said Alison firmly. She took her plaid from its peg. "I'll just tell my faither whaur we're gaun. He's oot the back. Dinnae fash yersel'," she added, seeing Bessie's stricken look. "He'll no hae heard us. When he's tendin' his kail he's deaf tae a' else."

*

Tom whiled away the afternoon sitting under the apple tree in the garden, idly turning the pages of the Scots Magazine. He had decided to slip away to Ayr when dusk fell and the family was finishing supper. He still had some hours to get through and mixed excitement and apprehension made it impossible to concentrate on reading. He was grateful when Kate appeared, sent by Jeanie to pick blackberries for a pie. She sat down beside Tom and began to plague him with questions.

"What's it like inside the Tolbooth?" she asked blithely.

Tom shivered at the memory of that grim place. "Ye dinnae want tae ken."

"Are there rats?"

"There are rats. It's filthy and damp and dark an' I dinnae want tae talk aboot it, seein' as I'll soon be back there."

Kate reddened, remembering.

"Sorry," she muttered, "I didnae mean tae . . ."

"Never mind."

There was an uneasy silence.

"Tom?"

"Aye?"

"What'll happen on Saturday?"

Tom had been wondering about that himself.

"I dinnae really ken," he said. "I suppose they'll come for me here if I dinnae gi'e myself up, then there'll be a trial at the next assizes, an' then . . ."

"But if ye're no guilty? They dinnae condemn innocent folk, dae they?"

Tom laughed bitterly. His wee sister was innocent of the ways of the world.

"It happens, whiles. If they dinnae find the murderer, an' naebody but us seems tae be tryin' tae dae that, I'm for it."

"Could ye no just gang awa'? What's tae stop ye?"

Tom admitted that it had crossed his mind. "But then they'd be sure I was guilty. I'd be an outlaw, no safe onywhaur. I'd need tae gang abroad. I could never come back here."

"An' forbye," he went on, "they'd think ye'd a' helped me, especially Faither. It'd be the ruin o' the family. I cannae dae that."

Kate sniffed. Looking at her, Tom saw one big tear rolling down her cheek. He stood up.

"Dinnae worry, wee sister. We've still got a few days. Noo, let's see aboot the blackberries."

*

In the early evening, David and Mungo arrived back from the fields, weary and content after a long day's work in the sunshine. Mungo was full of the joys of farming and indeed, as the family gathered for supper, he looked healthier and happier than Tom had ever seen him.

"I could get tae like this farmin' business," he said cheerfully as he tucked into a heaped plate of mutton stew.

"Aye, it's fine when the sun shines," agreed David. "If the weather hauds, we can maybe get some hay made soon."

"An' hoo's my new wee sister?" continued Mungo, turning to Kate, who was sitting beside him, and patting her arm. "Hae ye missed me the day?"

Kate blushed. "Oh aye," she muttered, looking uncertainly at Tom. *Wee sister* was his term of endearment.

Tom told himself not to mind. It was only Mungo's way; he was as insensitive to others as he was sensitive to his own needs. He meant no harm by it, and Tom tried not to think that come next week Mungo might well have taken his, Tom's, place in the family.

"We'll see hoo ye feel aboot farmin' when ye're howkin' tatties in the snell wind an' the rain," he said, but with a teasing smile. "It wasnae a pleasure for me."

"So ye went off tae France an' discovered mair intimate kinds o' pleasure," jeered Mungo with a wicked leer. No-one laughed. "Sorry," he mumbled. "I let my tongue get the better o' me, whiles."

"Let's see what Jeanie's got for pudding," said Lady Margaret quickly, "and hope it's no' tansy."

*

A short while later, Tom excused himself and went up to his room to get ready. He dressed in a plain dark jerkin and hose before creeping down the back stairs, tiptoeing past the kitchen where Jeanie was applying another mustard poultice to Bob's knee, and slipping out through the back door. He tied a rough woollen scarf round his neck and pulled an old felt hat over his head.

Dusk was falling and he reckoned that by the time he got to Ayr it would be dark enough to slip into the Cunningham yard unseen. The sky was clear and the evening still warm; Tom hoped there would be enough moonlight later to aid his task, for he dared not make any light.

He saw no-one in the country lanes as he walked steadily towards the town. All the country folk had finished their day's work and his only companions were a cloud of persistent midges and a lone whaup calling from the moors. As he reached the first houses of the town there were more folk about, hurrying home or towards the taverns, but no-one paid him any notice, taking him for just another working man heading home.

Before long he was standing in the gathering gloom in Cunningham's yard, at the foot of the stairs to the offices. He was tormented by memories of the last time he had stood here, a few short days before, seeing the light in the windows above. No light burned there now, and the yard was deserted. If he could go back in time to last Friday, would he still have climbed those stairs?

Tom shook off these thoughts and, ignoring the fear which made his legs tremble, mounted the stairs. The door was not locked. He entered his and Mungo's old lair. In the gloom, he could make out the door to the inner office, which stood ajar. He quickly crossed the room and went in, half expecting to see Richard Cunningham again, slumped in his lifeblood.

There was no body, of course; his employer's mortal remains had already been buried. Everything else seemed as it had been the last time Tom had stood here. He looked around, his task aided by the dim light from the quayside coming through the big windows. Some attempt had been made to clean up but the rug, the desk and the walls still bore rusty red bloodstains. Mr Cunningham's chair had been moved back against the wall, but the desk had not been touched. Tom went to examine it and was struck by the thought that something, normally there, was missing. The heavy onyx inkstand was in its usual place, alongside the neat row of pens and quills; a ledger lay open, showing through the bloodstains rows of figures in Mungo's neat hand, but there was no sign of the paper knife which had always lain on the desk. Richard Cunningham had told Tom that the small sharp knife, with its gold handle set with a single ruby, had been a present from his wife, and he kept it on his desk as a constant reminder of her.

Tom felt a wave of nausea. Had the knife been used to stab Cunningham? A quick search in the desk drawers confirmed its absence and the likelihood that it was, indeed, the murder weapon.

A sound from the courtyard made Tom start. A man's deep voice followed by a woman's low, flirtatious laugh, out of place in this house of death. Tom quickly crossed to a window in the clerks' office and looked out. Night had fallen but the moon was bright and by its light he could see two figures standing by the warehouse door, locked in a passionate embrace. As he watched, the man lifted his mouth from the woman's and Tom recognised him at once as Adam Kennedy.

Tom felt disgusted. Kennedy had always been arrogant, but now he was treating the warehouse as his personal domain, bringing his doxy there and God knew what else. He could not see who the woman was but her voice came again, caressingly.

"*Attends-moi, Adam. Je reviens.*" She turned away and the moonlight fell on the proud face of Isabelle Cunningham as she crossed the yard and disappeared out towards the quayside.

Tom was numbed by cold, sickening rage. "Whore!" he muttered. So much for the sorrowful widow, laid low by grief. She and Kennedy were obviously lovers, and her husband buried only two days before. Another thought struck him. How long had they been lovers? Had they plotted against Richard Cunningham, killed him even? He remembered what his father had said about motive and opportunity. Motive they certainly had, if they were lovers and meant to rid themselves of her husband; still more if she stood to inherit her husband's wealth. Opportunity too; Kennedy was often hanging around the warehouse at night and Tom remembered that Isabelle had been expected at the office on the evening of her husband's death. Had she killed him? Tom gripped the window-frame, shaken to the core.

Kennedy had by now disappeared into the stables and the yard was deserted. Time passed. At length the first wave of shock subsided and Tom debated what to do next. There was nothing more to be found in the offices, Kennedy was presumably still in the stables, and Isabelle had said she was coming back. Tom's instincts told him he should go home but he was determined to find out more, and he would never have another chance. He remembered what Bob had overheard from the McSkimmings. It seemed the smuggling was still going on – another reason to be rid of Richard Cunningham – and perhaps more openly now that he had gone. Tom decided to see if the warehouse held any more clues to their activities. If he could find out exactly what was going on, perhaps it was not too late to clear his name. An inner voice counselled caution. What if he were caught? He would stand no chance against

Kennedy and the McSkimmings. Tom pushed the thought firmly away.

He moved quietly down the steps to the deserted yard and made his way round the edge, in the shadow of the buildings. The small side door to the warehouse was unlocked and he slipped through. Not much had changed since he had last been there; the chests and crates were piled as high as ever, their bulk looming over him in the dim moonlight.

Tom walked up and down the central aisles then, wondering if goods were still stored in the secret cellar, he made his way over to the far wall where the stairs to the basement were. To his surprise there were no longer any chests hiding the secret door; it seemed that with Mr Cunningham, Mungo and himself no longer there, and the excise men not due to visit for several weeks, there was no more need for secrecy. The door stood open and Tom could distinguish the outline of the stone steps leading down.

Carefully, holding on to the wall for support, he groped his way down to the dark cellar. The weak moonlight coming through the high windows showed that there were still some chests and crates lying haphazardly about, but many had gone. There had obviously been an increase in distributing the smuggled goods over the past week, probably because they could now do it more openly.

Tom was just starting back up the steps when the door above him slammed shut and he heard the scrape of a key turning in the lock. He was caught, like a rat in a trap.

*

How long he had been sitting in the dark, cursing himself for a fool, he had no idea. Hours, it seemed, but it was probably only minutes. He had checked that the small windows high in the wall were too small for him to squeeze through. Had he been locked in accidentally or deliberately? He presumed the latter, which meant they would be coming back for him unless they meant to just leave him there to starve. Either way, he was done for. Tom swallowed hard, trying to beat down a rising wave of panic.

It was almost a relief when the door opened and the flash of a lantern lit up the stairs. Blinded by the light, he could not at first see who was there, but the tramp of heavy boots on the steps and the sound of mocking laughter soon told him it was Adam Kennedy and the McSkimmimg brothers.

"Weel noo, Master Boyd, curiosity gets the better o' ye again." Kennedy spoke quietly, shaking his head regretfully. "Tie him up, boys." A length of rope was produced and Geordie McSkimming, none too gently, tied his hands behind his back.

Kennedy raised the lantern to study his face. Tom could smell spirits on the other man's breath and the lantern wavered slightly. A loud, giggling belch from Wullie McSkimming confirmed that they were at that stage of drunkenness when men will do foolhardy things with no thought for the consequences.

"What are we gonnae dae wi' him, lads?" asked Kennedy. "We cannae let him get awa', he kens ower much aboot the business, it seems."

"We could chuck him in the harbour," said Wullie. "I'd quite like tae watch him droon."

"Naw, that tak's ower lang, an' somebody might see," said his brother. "We could just leave him here an' forget him. Shame he hasnae got the fancy coat on – it would look guid on a skeleton."

"Naw, he'd stink the place oot," said Kennedy. "The harbour, I think, but we'll need tae be quick. We'll slit his throat first, an' put stanes in his pockets so he doesnae float. You twa haud him still," he added, drawing a vicious-looking long-bladed knife from a sheath at his belt.

Rough hands seized Tom and he felt the sharp blade at his throat and Kennedy's whisky-sodden breath on his cheek. He closed his eyes and sent his last thoughts to Alison.

*

"Stop, Adam! What is the meaning of this?" cried a voice and, suddenly released, Tom stumbled and fell sharply against the wall as Isabelle Cunningham came quickly down the stairs.

"Untie him," she snapped. Wullie McSkimming hurried to obey and Tom, released, put a hand to his throat, where he felt the stickiness of blood. It seemed to be only a scratch. He dared not let himself think of what would have happened had Isabelle not intervened.

"This is madness," she said, in a tone which brooked no argument. "Why kill him now and have his blood on our hands when the law will do it for us in a few days' time?" She stepped closer to Tom, who was aware once more of her subtle French perfume and her icily beautiful smile. It was obvious that she was in command and that the three men would do her bidding, whatever that might be.

"Mon pauvre Tom," she said gently, drawing a finger slowly down his cheek and lightly tickling his chin. Beside him, Adam Kennedy muttered an oath and tightened his grip on the knife. Isabelle turned to him. "Ne t'inquiète pas, Adam," she said softly, "he is nothing to me. We will give him to the hangman. Now let us get out of this foul cellar," she added, wrinkling her nose prettily as she turned towards the stairs.

As he stumbled up the steps between the McSkimming brothers, Tom could feel waves of hostility and frustrated blood-lust coming from them. He realised he was not out of danger yet.

By the door of the main warehouse, Isabelle Cunningham turned once more to give orders to the men. "We will send to the Tolbooth and have the men of the watch come to take Mr Boyd there. Adam, will you do that? Geordie and Wullie, I want you to go down to the cellar and tidy everything up. It is a stinking mess down there, and I will not have that on my premises."

"What, an' leave you here wi' him?" jeered Kennedy.

She quelled him with a look. "I think," she said icily, "that unlike some others of my acquaintance, Mr Boyd is an honourable man. However, since you are worried, give me that piece of rope and I will bind his wrists."

She moved behind Tom and once again he was aware of her perfume and the cool touch of her hands as she fastened the rope.

"Now go," she ordered.

Kennedy ran out of the warehouse, stumbling in his haste, while the McSkimmings stomped off towards the cellar. Muttered oaths could be heard as they scrambled down the steps and began shoving crates and barrels around.

"Quickly," hissed Isabelle, "we don't have much time." As Tom stood bewildered, she whispered, "I know you did not kill my husband, and before you ask, neither did I. I do not wish to see you hanged, so before they come back I want you to free yourself – the knots are loose – and go before the watch gets here."

"But they'll ken if ye let me go," said Tom, slipping his wrists free of the knots.

"Not if you knock me down."

"I cannae dae that."

"You must."

Tom stared at her. Was there anyone who refused to do her bidding?

"Just one thing," he said. "Kennedy. I saw ye baith. How could ye?"

"*C'est le commerce,*" she said with a shrug. "I must survive as I can. Now hit me and go, as fast as you can."

Tom hesitated, then gave her a half-hearted shove. Isabelle immediately let out a blood-curdling scream and threw herself to the floor.

Below them, Tom could hear the McSkimmings begin to rush up the steps so he ran for the door.

Outside in the yard, he paused briefly to make sure Kennedy was not already back, then he ran fast to the quayside and hurried along towards the bridge, keeping to the shadows by the walls.

Reaching the end of the quay, he heard the sound of hurried, tramping feet and slipped down on to the river bank, seeking what shelter he could under the bridge. He crouched down and held his breath as the armed men thundered across the bridge above him, sure the loud pounding of his heart would betray him. Sure enough, the footsteps paused and the voice of the captain floated down. "I thocht I saw something moving doon there. Bring the torches closer."

For what seemed an eternity, Tom crouched as motionless as he could, fighting a desire to sneeze.

"Should we gang doon there, sir?" asked one man as he swung his torch back and forth in an effort to see.

"There's nothing there, an' we've nae time to lose," came Kennedy's impatient voice. "Hurry up there." Tom breathed a sigh of relief as the men moved off the bridge and along the quay.

He made his way back up to the bridge, hurried across and down the vennel to the High Street where, keeping his head down, he moved as quickly as he dared without drawing attention to himself, mingling with the late revellers leaving the taverns. Only when he reached the outskirts of the town did he dare to slow down. His legs were shaking and his heart still pounding as his brain tried to make sense of all that had happened.

CHAPTER 20

Thursday September 6th

Tom woke from confused dreams of knives, ropes and Isabelle Cunningham's mocking smile. Sounds drifted up from the courtyard below – the cheerful laughter of David and Mungo going off to the fields, the clucking of hens and the authoritative voice of Jeanie supervising the first jam-making of the season. Tom sighed and went back to sleep.

When he awoke again the sun was high in the sky and there was no noise from below. He quickly washed, dressed and hurried downstairs in search of breakfast. The dining-room was deserted so he headed for the kitchen.

"My, you're up early," said Jeanie sarcastically. "Ye'll be wanting some breakfast. There's some parritch an' bannocks; there were eggs and kippers but they were feenished three hours since."

"Morning, Jeanie," said Tom, settling himself with a mug of ale and prodding at the now leathery porridge.

Jeanie brought over oatcakes and cheese. "When ye've finished, your faither wants tae see ye in his study."

Tom groaned. If his father summoned him to his study, it always meant trouble.

His fears were confirmed ten minutes later when he took a seat opposite his father, who sat with steepled fingers and a stern expression behind his imposing desk.

"Whaur were ye yestreen?" demanded his sire without preamble.

Tom opened his mouth to deny going out, but something in Sir Malcolm's level gaze told him it would be useless to lie.

"I ... I went intae Ayr," he muttered, expecting an explosion of rage. None came.

"And ...?"

"I went tae Cunningham's."

"And ...?"

Tom found himself reliving the events of the previous evening as he recited the whole sorry tale to his father. When he finished there was a heavy silence.

"I'm sorry, faither. I shouldnae hae done it."

Sir Malcolm harrumphed.

"Weel, it's done noo, an' at least ye're hame in one piece. Did ye at least learn onything?"

"Aye, I think so," began Tom uncertainly. "I had a guid look at Mr Cunningham's desk, tae see if I'd remembered it richt, an' I definitely didnae see his paper knife. He used it for opening letters an' peelin' apples an' it aye sat on his desk. It was a fancy Italian knife wi' a gold jewelled handle. I couldnae find it; it wasnae in the drawers either."

"So it might hae been used on him an' the murderer took it awa' efterwards. Ocht else?"

"I couldnae fathom Mrs Cunningham's game. She helped me escape, in fact she saved my life, but she's in cahoots wi' Kennedy and his gang." Tom grimaced, remembering the cold rasp of steel at his throat.

"Maybe she has been all along, or maybe they're forcing her tae go along wi' them."

"I dinnae think so," said Tom, thinking of Isabelle Cunningham's imperious ways. "She's the one callin' the shots. They sent for the watch, an' if she hadnae helped me I'd be back in the Tolbooth. What'll happen noo?" he added fearfully.

"Depends. The watchmen could come here for ye, but if they're busy they'll likely wait till Saturday. Either way, ye'll need tae gang awa.'"

"Awa'?"

"Aye. Ye mind I went tae Ayr on Tuesday?"

"Aye. Ye wouldnae let me gang wi' ye."

"Weel, I went tae see a merchant I ken, wha owes me money

for defending him in court an' never paid me. He has a cargo leavin' for Ireland the morn's nicht an' there's a place for ye on the ship."

Tom was dumbfounded. His father, the most upstanding and incorruptible lawyer of his generation, was going to break the law for him. Sir Malcolm had given his word to deliver Tom to the Sheriff on Saturday. If the truth were known, and it surely would be, it would end his career and probably ruin the family.

"No, faither. I cannae let ye dae that."

"You will, Thomas," said his father in a tone which brooked no argument. "I cannae let ye be hanged for something ye didnae dae. It would break your mither's heart ... an' mine tae," he added quietly.

Tom was silent as he considered the implications. He wouldn't hang, unless they caught him, but he would be an outlaw with a price on his head. He would have to live in exile, never seeing his family, or Alison, again.

"No, faither," he said again. "I cannae dae it. It would be the ruin o' ye, an' I'd never see ye again. I'd rather face things here."

"Thomas, my boy, we've had a week an' we're nane the wiser. If they try ye, they'll surely hang ye. This way, ye stay alive an' we still hae some hope."

"Ye say ye arranged it on Tuesday, but you've never said ocht aboot it till noo."

"I still hoped we could find wha killed Mr Cunningham, but it doesnae look like we will, noo. So the morn's nicht ye'll gang tae Dunure tae get on the ship."

"Dunure?"

"Aye. It's ower risky for ye tae gang on board at Ayr. There's aye a wheen o' folk on the quays – including your friends frae Cunningham's – an' the watch'll be lookin' for ye, so ye're tae gang tae Dunure. The ship'll lie off for half an hour after midnight. Ye'll need tae signal frae the castle an' they'll send a wee boat for ye. If ye dinnae show up by half past twelve they'll sail withoot ye, so mind ye get there on time."

"Is that why we went tae Dunure yesterday?"

"Aye. I wanted tae remind mysel' o' the lie o' the land."

"Does my mither ken?"

"Aye, but naebody else. There's time enough tae tell them later on."

Tom spent the next few hours coming to terms with the possibility that he would perhaps live beyond the following week, but would never see his loved ones again, or at least not for many years. Above all, he longed to see Alison just once more.

The McFadzean aunts had been invited for tea at four o'clock, a prospect which did nothing to raise Tom's spirits. Bob fetched them by carriage and when they arrived, in a flurry of gay silks and nodding plumes, it was obvious they were in a state of high excitement.

"My dears!" exclaimed Miss Effie. "Ye'll never guess ..."

"Sic a to-do! I've never heard the like!" added Miss Letty.

Lady Margaret managed to persuade them to postpone telling their news until tea had been served, and as the weather was fine, the tea-table was set up on the lawn behind the house, where Jeanie and one of the maids served scones and pound cake to the assembled family. Kate was banished, under protest, to the kitchen, where she would be allowed extra cake to compensate for being excluded from the family discussion. She comforted herself with the knowledge that whatever juicy gossip her aunts had to impart would be well known to Jeanie, who would lose no time in telling her, and likely include some extra details.

Once Kate had gone, the sisters embarked with relish on their tale.

"It's a' ower the toon!" said Miss Effie.

"The mercat's fair buzzin' wi' it," added Miss Letty.

"Of course, ye dinnae want tae believe a' ye hear..."

"But when ye hae a reliable source, as we have, ye have tae gi'e it some credence."

"This is fascinating," said Sir Malcolm, "but what exactly are we talkin' aboot?"

"Mr Cunningham . . ." began Miss Effie.

"Mr James, the kirk elder, no Mr Richard, who was murdered . . . ." added her sister helpfully.

" . . . was called tae see the minister!"

"Is that unusual?" enquired Lady Margaret.

"Oh aye, the minister's maid heard everything . . ."

" . . . and she tellt Maisie!" added Miss Letty, naming their own maid.

"Of course," sniffed Miss Effie, "I ken better than tae aye believe servants' gossip . . ."

" . . . but in this case it seems tae be true. An' him an elder o' the kirk. Wickedness!"

Tom began to see what they were hinting at.

"What has Mr Cunningham done, Aunt Effie?" he asked.

"Twa lassies went to see the minister yestreen . . . .." began Miss Effie.

" . . . and accused Mr Cunningham of . . ." here Miss Letty looked around, and dropped her voice dramatically, "fornication!"

"But surely the minister wouldnae believe them!" This from Lady Margaret. "More tea, Effie?"

"In a minute. Weel, ye'd think sae, but one o' the lassies was Bessie Gibney . . ."

" . . . an' she took her twa black-haired weans wi' her. The minister had never seen them afore, an' he had tae admit there was quite a resemblance tae Mr Cunningham."

Miss Letty took up the tale.

"But what really convinced the minister was the ither lassie . . ."

"Wha was that?" asked Tom, thinking he probably already knew the answer.

"Mistress Alison Fleming!" pronounced Miss Effie with relish. "She said he'd tried tae ... force her, on the Sabbath, in her ain back shop! I must say I've nae reason tae think the lassie's lyin', I've aye found her decent and honest, but it's hard tae believe Mr Cunningham would dae that."

"He did, though," said Tom mildly.

"Aye," said his mother, "we kent that already. How brave of Mistress Fleming tae gang tae the minister."

Miss Effie was disappointed that her juiciest item of gossip seemed to be known by her listeners already, and briefly wondered how they had come by this knowledge. She soon recovered however.

"So it seems it's true," she said. "Mind you, I've aye thocht there was something no' quite right aboot yon man."

"Aye, I mind him looking at my ankles mair than once," added her sister with a satisfied shudder.

"What'll happen noo?" asked Tom.

"Weel," said Sir Malcolm, "nothin's been proved; there's only the accusation. He'll have to answer for it tae the Kirk Session."

"I expect Alison's testimony will carry a lot o' weight," said Lady Margaret. "She has nae reason tae lie."

And I could back her up, as a witness to the attack, thought Tom, then remembered that he would be far away long before the case came up.

Just as finally the talk was turning to other subjects Bob appeared from the back of the stables to announce the arrival of Alison Fleming herself. Miss Effie and Miss Letty practically bounced with excitement, making Tom think of two parrots on a perch.

Alison crossed the lawn and sat down, gratefully accepting the offer of tea. Tom, who had thought he would never see her again, drank in the sight of her, thinking how cool and lovely she looked in her simple blue dress and muslin fichu, her hair bound up in an Indian silk scarf. Alison, for her part, was casting round for a reason to explain her uninvited visit. She could hardly say she just wanted to see Tom one last time.

Tom was trying hard not to stare at her, remembering that she had parted in anger from him at their last meeting. Just then she looked up, and her quick smile reassured him.

Greetings over, the Misses McFadzean could contain their curiosity no longer.

"Mistress Fleming, is it true what they say?"

"Did ye gang tae the minister?"

"Did Mr Cunningham ...?" here Miss Effie stopped, at a loss for a suitably polite word to describe what she meant.

"Effie, Letty," said Lady Margaret, "these are personal matters."

Alison seized the opportunity.

"It's quite alright, ma'am," she said, "I understand that everyone is shocked and they want an explanation for these events. In fact that's why I came; tae tell ye myself what happened, rather than have ye learn it through hearsay." She took care not to look at the Misses McFadzean.

"Ye dinnae owe us ony explanation, my lass," said Sir Malcolm. "We're just pleased tae see ye, as always."

"Nevertheless, I'd like tae explain." She quickly recounted how she had befriended Bessie Gibney and how, knowing that Alison too had been attacked by him, Bessie had reluctantly decided to name James Cunningham and had enlisted her help. They had gone together to the minister, who had listened patiently to their tale but had made no comment other than sighing deeply and assuring them that he would look into the matter. Alison had heard later that James Cunningham had been interviewed by the minister and summoned to appear before the Kirk Session the following week.

The Misses McFadzean, disappointed that Alison's account had not included graphic details of how Cunningham had tried to ravish her in her own workroom, turned to speculation.

"Will ye have tae attend the session, Mistress Fleming?"

"Will ony mair lassies come forward?"

"Dae ye think they'll find him guilty?"

"He'll be disgraced."

"Will he have tae stand in the kirk? I'd like tae see that," said Miss Effie with relish.

Tom thought that he, too, would like to see that, although for different reasons, but he was grateful for Alison's sake when Lady Margaret steered the conversation into other, safer waters. He had been hoping that he would have a chance to speak to Alison in private and when she rose to take her leave he quickly offered to accompany her to the gate.

They walked around to the stable yard in silence. Alison untethered her donkey and by unspoken agreement they went through the gate into the walled garden.

"Sorry..." began Tom.

"I'm sorry..." began Alison simultaneously.

They both laughed and the tension eased.

"We didnae part on the best o' terms last time," said Alison, "but I understand why, an' I'm sorry I was angry. How are things wi' ye noo?"

Tom found himself relating his encounter of the previous evening with Isabelle Cunningham and the Kennedy gang. Alison listened quietly but her face grew more and more anxious as he spoke. When he had finished, she sighed deeply.

"Ye were daft tae dae it, Tom. They could hae killed ye."

"I've no' a lot left tae lose," said Tom. "We've found oot naethin' mair." He told her then about Bob's adventure on the docks and his suspicions that the gang had killed Richard Cunningham.

"I cannae believe Mrs Cunningham's involved," said Alison. "It disnae mak' sense. She lives her life her ain way, and she's no' a saint, but she's hardly a Jezebel. I cannae see her having a hand in her husband's death and gi'ing up her position for the likes o' Adam Kennedy."

"Maybe he has some kind o' hold over her."

"But what? From what ye say, it sounds like she ca's the shots in their relationship."

"Aye, an' a guid thing for me, as it turned oot," said Tom ruefully.

Alison thought for a moment.

"James Cunningham," she said at last. "Could it be him that killed his brither?"

"I've thocht an' thocht aboot this. He came on the scene very quickly, him that normally never gangs near the office. But why would he dae it?"

"Maybe Richard threatened tae expose him. They grew up thegither an' Richard kent his character. He must hae kent he was a fornicator."

"But why noo? James has been daein' it for years."

"Maybe he'd just seen him defile ower mony lassies, an' Bessie Gibney having tae stand in the kirk again was the last straw."

They fell silent. After a week of investigation all they had was speculation and it was getting them nowhere. Tom was aware of time passing, of how little they had left.

"Alison . . ." he began.

She looked up at him, her grey eyes full of concern.

He told her about his father's decision, about the ship he would take from Dunure the following night.

"I'm glad there's a way oot for ye," she said simply.

"But I'll be an exile. I dinnae ken if I'll ever be able tae come back."

"So this is goodbye?" She tried to keep her voice steady, but he could hear the despair in it.

"It seems so. I'd gi'e onything for it tae be otherwise."

"We could write. Would ye write tae me, Tom?"

"I will. I promise I'll write, even if my letters never reach ye."

"I will too."

A moment's silence.

"Alison . . ." he said uncertainly.

"Aye...?"

"Could... could I hae a kiss from ye afore I go?"

She smiled. "Of course."

She stood on tiptoe and reached up. He felt the cool sweet touch of her lips on his, all too briefly, and the salt tang of tears, though whether they were hers or his, he could not say.

"Fare thee weel, Tom," she whispered.

A long last look, then she pulled her reluctant donkey through the gate, mounted and rode away.

As he came out of the garden, his heart heavy and his head full of thoughts of Alison, he bumped into David and Mungo coming back from the fields.

"Hoo are ye, Tom? Enjoyin' yer last days o' freedom?" asked Mungo. Tom tried not to be resentful, for he knew now to take such clumsy remarks at face value. Mungo really was enquiring after his welfare, not meaning to remind him how short a time was left to him.

"Aye, we've just had the McFadzean aunties here for tea an' a gossip. Maybe I'll no' miss that," he added with an attempt at cheerfulness.

*

After supper Sir Malcolm and Tom outlined to the family their plans for Tom's escape. They did not go into details in case the family were questioned later; the less they knew the better. All were relieved that Tom had a chance to escape the gallows, but the thought of his being an outlaw was hard to bear, especially as his escape would be seen as an admission of guilt. No-one mentioned the possible ruin of the family; one look at Sir Malcolm's face convinced them that argument was useless, even had they wanted to raise it.

Later, as Tom made his way back to his room, he was waylaid by Mungo.

"So ye're runnin' awa'," he began with his usual lack of tact.

"I dinnae seem tae hae a choice."

"But if ye didnae dae it..."

Tom sighed and said nothing. He had had this discussion so many times before.

"What aboot me?" cried Mungo.

"You? But ye'll be fine. Ye like the farm work, ye get on fine wi' David and Kate, ye'll be able tae stay here. An' ye'll can see yer mither when ye want tae."

If only I had that luxury, he added to himself.

"Ye dinnae understand," said Mungo. "I'm in mortal fear a' the time."

"The smugglers? If they were gonnae dae onything tae ye they'd hae done it by noo. Ye just need tae keep yer heid doon an' no gang near Cunningham's."

"They're just bidin' their time, maist like."

In vain Tom tried to allay the other man's fears. Finally Mungo burst out, "Can ye no' see, Tom. I cannae spend my life in fear. I need tae gang awa', far awa'. Tak' me wi' ye ... please."

Tom had little enough relish for the future as it was; the thought of a lifetime in exile with Mungo dogging his steps was too much to bear. He tried to think of a diplomatic way out.

"Whaur would ye gang?" he asked.

"I dinnae ken. What aboot you?"

"Weel, Ireland first." Perhaps he could lose Mungo in a peat bog in the wilds of Kerry. "Then I thocht I might gang back tae France."

"France. I'd like that fine. I like tae hear ye talk o' it ... and Madeleine."

Tom realised that he had not thought of Madeleine for a long time.

"Or maybe the Americas if ... when ... the colonists win the war."

"Aye," agreed Mungo, "We'd be safe there."

Safe? thought Tom. *In a wild unknown country where the British weren't welcome?*

"So ye'll tak' me wi' ye?"

"I havenae said that. Are ye sure ye want tae gang sae far awa'?"

"The further the better. I cannae stand aye lookin' ower my shoother in case there's a gowk ahint me wi' a knife."

"But ye've seemed a lot happier these past days."

"Aye, I've liked workin' wi' Davie. Fresh air, sunshine, physical work. I'm mair at peace then."

"Then why no stay? My family would welcome ye. Kate's fond o' ye."

"Aye, she's a grand lass." Mungo's sharp features softened for a moment. "But I need tae gang awa'. If Kennedy an' his crew can dae awa' wi' Mr Cunningham they can kill me an a'. Please, Tom. I'll no bother ye once we're awa' frae here. Ye can tell me tae get lost then. Please . . . I'm beggin' ye."

Tom did not reply immediately. It might be that he would welcome company when he set off; it would be a lonely road to travel on his own.

"I'm no' sure they can tak' twa," he said. "My faither arranged it. I dinnae ken what he's paid the captain."

"I've got some money saved up. If I can just get tae the ship I hope I'll can persuade the captain."

"Weel, maybe. We can try, anyway."

Mungo's face lit up. "I'm feelin' better already. Thanks, Tom. I kent ye'd let me come."

Tom didn't know where this certainty came from.

"Let's get some sleep," he said. "We'll need it." But he knew he'd find it hard to sleep for the last time in his own bed.

CHAPTER 21

Friday September 7th

Tom rose early after a restless night. He washed quickly and tidied his bed, wondering where he would lay his head that evening. He looked round the room which had been his since he was ten years old, thinking it had always been good to come back here after university and then after his time in France. He had his books, some well-thumbed, read and loved again and again, others, such as his mathematics textbooks and some volumes on the law, neglected and gathering dust. He opened a drawer containing some forgotten scrapbooks and his collection of toy soldiers, but a great lump came to his throat and he closed the drawer quickly.

Outside the window the day was bright and sunny, with the heat already building up. It was a shame to be leaving now, he thought, after the dreich wet summer. He pushed such thoughts firmly to the back of his mind and went in search of breakfast. For once, he was not late. The family was gathered in the small dining room where Jeanie was serving porridge and kippers. There was a short silence as he took his seat, before everyone started making determinedly cheerful conversation. Mungo was there too, looking tense; Tom doubted he had slept much either.

"Ye'll be coming wi' me tae the farm as usual, Mungo?" asked David. "We can maybe mak' some hay the day."

"Weel, maybe till noon. I'll need tae gang an' see my mither efter."

"Oh really? Can it no wait? We've a wheen o' work tae dae while the weather hauds."

"I thocht I should gang an' say fareweel tae my mither. I'll like as no' never see her again." Seeing the puzzled faces around the table he added, "Did Tom no' tell ye? I'm gaun wi' him."

"What's this?" asked Sir Malcolm.

Tom coloured, and explained that Mungo had asked to go with him and he had agreed.

"What? An' jeopardise the whole enterprise?" roared his father. "What were ye thinkin', Tom?"

"Please, Sir Malcolm," Mungo ventured, "don't blame Tom. He thocht it best tae gang alone, but I persuaded him tae tak' me. If the captain'll let me aboard," he added, quaking a little under Sir Malcolm's piercing gaze.

Sir Malcolm said nothing, merely continued to stare. Mungo stammered on, "I need tae gang awa', for the smugglers is efter me. I'm feart a' the time. I've got siller saved up," he added. "I can pay my way, an' mair." His voice tailed off.

Sir Malcolm stared at the two youths for some time, then sighed and said, "Very well, I'll leave it up tae Tom. But if ye dae ocht at a' tae harm my son's chances o' escape, ye'll hae me tae answer tae, an' I doot there'll be much left o' ye when I'm feenished."

Tom spoke up quickly. "I can trust Mungo, faither. We've aye managed afore." He tried not to think of how Mungo had nearly got them both drowned. "We'll be fine. Forbye, I'd be glad o' company."

His father stared at him for what seemed an age before muttering, "Humph, aye, weel . . ."

No more was said.

*

Tom spent the morning roaming around the house and gardens, his mood alternating between impatience to be off and the desire to savour the last bitter-sweet hours in his childhood home.

Noon found him on the main staircase, in front of the portraits of his ancestors. He had never examined them closely; as a child he had always run past them, his gaze averted, afraid of the eyes which seemed to follow him. Now, curiosity prompted him to look more closely and read the inscriptions under each painting.

Sir Edward Boyd (1290-1347), companion of Bruce at the Battle of Bannockburn.

Sir Edward wore chain mail and a long drooping moustache and wielded a battle-axe stained, no doubt, with the blood of Englishmen.

Sir Robert Boyd of Dalmeny (1475-1530), court poet to James IV.

Sir Robert, dressed in fine silks and strumming a lute, gazed out of the frame with an expression somewhere between dreamy and martial.

Lady Mary Boyd (1542-1600), lady-in-waiting to Queen Mary.

Lady Mary was soberly dressed in black, but her fine blonde curls spoke of a flirtatious nature slightly at odds with her simpering expression of patient forbearance acquired through years of suffering the caprices of her royal mistress.

The Reverend Ebenezer Boyd (1605-1679), minister of the Reformed Church.

The Reverend Boyd, stood in his pulpit, his unkempt grey hair trailing on his white starched collar. He held a Bible in one hand and the other was raised to heaven as he railed against sinners in general and Episcopalian bishops in particular.

Sir Nathaniel Boyd (1650-1719), sea captain, about to set sail for Darien.

Sir Nathaniel, a fine figure of a man, stood on the deck of his ship, one hand on the rigging, the other holding a large cutlass. His gaze managed to fix itself simultaneously on the spectator and on the distant horizon vaguely visible in the background.

"So you're takin' leave o' your ancestors," said his father beside him. Tom started. He had not heard Sir Malcolm approach.

"I've never looked at them properly afore," he confessed.

"They're an interesting bunch. I never realised there was so much history in the family. This yin," he added, pointing to the Reverend Ebenezer, "looks a lot like you."

"It is me," said his father mildly.

"An' this yin ... what did ye say?"

"That yin's me an' a'. They're a' me."

"Even Lady Mary, lady-in-waiting to Queen Mary?"

"Aye, that was the worst. Thon wig had fleas."

Looking again, Tom could see that beneath the simpering expression, Lady Mary had a distinctly masculine cast of features.

"Dae ye mean nane o' these folk existed?" he asked.

"They did ... in a way. I got the names and dates frae the family Bible, but I made up the rest."

Seeing that his son still looked puzzled, Sir Malcolm said, "I'd better tell ye the truth, but dinnae tell yer mither. She thinks they're genuine."

"So where dae they come frae?"

"When I was a student in Edinburgh, I had a friend, Roddy Crawford, who fancied himsel' as a portrait painter. He had a bit o' talent, but he was a great one for the drink. He got a chance o' an apprenticeship, but he had tae provide some samples o' his work. He didnae hae onything suitable, so we thocht this up between us. He borrowed some costumes and wigs frae an actor friend an' I made up the stories. It worked an' a'. He was ta'en on."

"I can see noo they're a' you, an' they're weel done, but how come ye look sae fierce in them a', even ..." he looked again at the inscription, " ... Sir Robert the court poet?"

"Aye, weel, it took us three weeks. Efter each session my airse was numb an' I'd a drouth on me like Saint Anthony in the desert. Nae wonder I looked scunnert."

When he had stopped laughing, Tom realised that he would miss his father, very much.

*

At five in the afternoon Alison was standing in her workroom, her heart heavy, full of thoughts of Tom and their parting. Any joy at discovering their shared feelings for each other was overlaid by the heavy pall of the knowledge that they might never meet again, or at least not for many years, when they would both be different people.

She was trying to work on Lady Margaret's gown, thinking that at least it gave her some connection to Tom, but she could not concentrate, always wondering what Tom was doing and thinking at that moment. How would it be in the coming days and weeks when she would still be sending all her thoughts to him, but with no idea where he was or what he was doing. Or even if he was still alive ... no, she would not think of that.

The sound of the shop door opening roused her from her reverie and she went quickly through to the front, glad of the distraction. On the threshold she stopped in surprise. Isabelle Cunningham was pacing back and forth, dramatic in her elegant black mourning, trailing expensive perfume.

"Mistress Fleming," she said without preamble, "I believe you came to see me last Sunday."

"Good-day, Madam. Yes, I did," replied Alison, puzzled. "I wished only to offer my condolences."

"And perhaps to question me on young Master Boyd's behalf." She held up a hand. "No, don't deny it. I know you visit his family and I would imagine you have developed some friendly feelings for that young man, especially given his present predicament. Am I right?"

"Well ..." Alison blushed, tongue-tied for once.

"I think you've just confirmed it," said Isabelle with a complacent smile. "Let me tell you that I share your admiration for Master Thomas, if not quite in the same way." That smile again, with a hint of mockery this time. "So I have some information which you may be able to use."

"Information?" Alison felt foolish, having no idea what this information might be. She still suspected Isabelle of complicity in her husband's death.

"You may have been told that I went to my husband's office on the night of his death," went on Isabelle. "Perhaps you wonder why?"

Alison could think of nothing to say.

"My husband sent for me because he had found some errors in the accounts and he wished to ask my opinion. There were indeed some anomalies; bank receipts for sums rather lower than those which appeared in the accounts and which we believed had been deposited. Small differences, hardly noticeable, but this had been going on for some time and taken together add up to a considerable amount of embezzlement." She looked at Alison keenly. "I believe you keep your father's books, so you will understand what I am saying."

"But who ...?" stammered Alison.

"Not Thomas, certainly; it started a long time ago. For a while, the sums stolen were infinitesimal, but the culprit got careless."

"So, it would be ... Mungo?"

"You have named him. My husband and I discussed what was to be done, and he reluctantly agreed with me that we would have to dismiss him. Richard was too soft-hearted for his own good, but it had to be done. He was going to tell Mungo the next day."

"And ... did ye leave then?"

"I did. That was the last time I saw my husband," said Isabelle, shaking her head in sorrow.

The two women were silent for a moment. Then Isabelle said, "I leave this knowledge with you, to use as you see fit. I assure you it is true." With that she turned and left the shop, leaving Alison speechless and confused.

She went through to the workroom and sat by the table, wondering what to do for the best. Could she trust what Isabelle had said? Perhaps it was an elaborate lie designed to cover her own guilt, or that of someone she was protecting, or perhaps she believed Mungo was guilty of her husband's murder.

Alison pondered this possibility. Mungo certainly had motive and opportunity if he had gone back to the office that night and learned he was to be dismissed. But was he capable of murder? Her knowledge of Mungo's character was drawn from her dealings with Annie and Tom; she had had little to do with him personally. She suspected his boastfulness and sharp tongue concealed a deep unease and fear of others, and that his moods swung rapidly between extremes, but could he really have killed an employer he was fond of?

"I'll go and see Annie," she thought, and before she could change her mind she had snatched up her plaid and was out the door.

She soon realised she could have left her plaid at home. The day was close and warm, the sky a queer leaden colour, the clouds tinged with coppery red. "Storm coming later," she thought.

She hurried through streets full of folk making their way home from market or towards the taverns. In Mill Street the stench from the tannery and breweries was stronger than ever, catching at her throat and almost making her retch.

Arriving at Annie's hovel she knocked firmly, hoping that Annie would be at home and in a lucid state, but afraid too. What if Mungo were there?

There was no answer to her repeated knocks, so she carefully pressed the latch and entered. The air inside was close and clammy and in the dim light she could see Annie sitting on a low stool by the cheerless hearth, nursing a bottle. She was already in her cups; all that Alison had achieved in weeks of patient care and encouragement had been undone.

"Annie," she said, "what's wrong?"

"Oh, it's you, bonnie lass," mumbled Annie. "Are ye gonnae mak' me a bite tae eat? I cannae seem tae get the fire lit the day."

Alison sighed, took off her plaid and set herself quickly to the task. Once the fire was lit, water for tea on the boil and a hasty meal of bannocks and rather mouldy cheese assembled and set in front of Annie, she sat down opposite her and pondered what to do next. Judging by her state, Annie had probably not seen her son for several days now that he was lodging with the Boyds, and worry and loneliness had obviously made her reach for the bottle again.

"Oh Annie," she thought, *"what am I gonnae dae wi' ye?"*

Alison told herself to be patient and wait until Annie was in a fit state to answer questions. Gradually some colour returned to her cheeks and she began to look brighter. Alison rose and began to tidy the room, noticing that at least Annie now slept in the box bed and not on the miserable heap of straw in the corner.

Deciding that she could at least clear out and replace the straw, she approached the heap with some trepidation. As she grasped the first armful of straw she saw something gleam in the dim light and reaching down, discovered a knife; a paper knife with a smooth edge and a wickedly sharp point. It had a beautiful ivory handle inlaid with gold and a single ruby which seemed to catch fire in the dim room, a knife such as Annie or Mungo could never have dreamed of owning.

"Annie," she said uncertainly, "what's this?"

Annie looked round. "I dinnae ken. Somethin' Mungo'll hae brocht hame. He's aye bringin' things frae the office."

Alison looked at the knife again and her blood ran cold. All along the blade were dull, rust-coloured marks, and there were more traces of the stuff in the stinking straw where it had been hidden. Richard Cunningham's lifeblood, she was sure. In the midst of her horror, Alison was certain of one thing. It was Mungo who had killed Richard.

Carefully, she replaced the knife where she had found it and pulled the straw over it. "When did ye last see Mungo?" she asked, trying to make her voice sound normal, though inside she was shaking with fear.

"Mungo? Did I no' say? He was here the noo, just afore ye came."

That was a surprise. "What did he say?"

"What dae ye want tae ken for?"

"I'm sorry, Annie, I dinnae mean tae pry into your business, but it's important. How was he?"

Annie blinked, swallowed, then drew herself up on her stool. She had obviously rehearsed what she said next.

"My son came tae tak' his leave o' me. He's gone abroad tae seek fame and fortune, then he'll come back for me."

"Abroad?"

"Aye. He's takin' ship the nicht, frae Dunure. It's a' arranged."

Dunure? But that was where Tom would be leaving from in a few hours' time. Surely Mungo wasn't going too? Thinking about it, Alison realised it made sense. That was why Mungo had been so frightened. It wasn't just the smugglers he feared; he was afraid the truth would be discovered. If Tom were hanged for murder, he would be safe, but if Tom escaped abroad, Mungo would live in constant fear. *"And rightly so,"* she thought, *"I have the proof here."* Suddenly it was important to get to Barnessie and tell what she knew before Tom left. She would leave the knife hidden; it could be collected later.

There was no time to lose. Alison stood up and was making for the door when she realised Annie was still talking.

"So I thocht if he went abroad I'd maybe never see him again, so I tellt him wha his faither was. He has a right tae ken."

Alison paused by the door. Could this be important? A thought struck her.

"Ye said ye were in service wi' a rich family in Ayr when ye were a lass."

"Aye, an' Mungo's faither was the son o' the hoose," said Annie proudly. "He'd hae merrit me an' a', if his besom o' a mither hadnae turned me oot."

Alison hesitated, but decided to ask.

"Was it the Cunninghams?"

"Aye. Oh, he was grand, my bonnie lad."

"James Cunningham? Did he seduce you an' a'?"

"James? Yon black corbie, aye peekin' roon corners an' fingerin' the lassies? Nae fear. Naw, it was his brither Richard, my bonnie laddie."

Alison held on to the door post for support, scarcely able to countenance the horror. Mungo, all unknowingly, had killed his own father.

"Aye, I tellt him," went on Annie blithely. "He didnae look ower pleased. Whaur are ye gaun, bonnie lass?"

CHAPTER 22

Alison ran back along Mill Street and through the High Street to the Sandgate, scarcely aware of the curious stares and some lewd calls from the men in the streets. Back home she untethered Jinty and called a quick farewell to her father before mounting and setting off as fast as she could towards the south. She knew she had to get to Barnessie before Tom and Mungo left for Dunure. The sky had darkened and she heard rumbles of distant thunder. The first fat raindrops were falling now; the storm had arrived.

*

Tom was taking leave of his family, trying to concentrate on being positive although his heart was breaking. He hardly dared look at his mother and Kate for fear of crying, and was grateful for the presence of his father, who concentrated on practical matters.

"Bob'll ride wi' ye tae Dunure an' bring back the horses," said Sir Malcolm. "Mind ye stay by the castle and look out for the signal. The ship'll no' wait if ye're late." He glared at Mungo, still unhappy about his part in the enterprise. Tom was increasingly doubtful about taking him along; since he had come back from seeing his mother in Ayr Mungo was in a state of nervous impatience and was barely coherent in his farewells. He ignored Kate completely, much to her sorrow, and did not utter a word of thanks to Lady Margaret for her hospitality.

"Come on, Tom, we maun gang," he said, making for the stable yard where Bob was waiting with the horses.

Tom embraced his mother and sister, gently disengaging himself when they clung to him, and exchanged long looks full of meaning with his father and David.

"Ride carefully," said Lady Margaret. "This weather's filthy."

Big drops of rain were falling as they mounted, and the storm wind was rustling in the trees. A flash of lightning lit up the scene for a moment and then the riders were lost from sight.

"Come awa' inside," said Jeanie. "I'll make us a' a hot toddy. Aye, you an' a', Kate, if yer mither agrees. One thing though, I'm no' sorry yon Mungo's gone. He's a sair trial tae honest folk."

*

Alison was making slow progress. The more she tried to hurry, the more Jinty seemed to resent it. It was tough going against the wind which whipped up mud and fallen leaves into her face and the rain which soaked through her clothes and numbed her hands so that she could scarcely grip the reins. It was dark by now and she had only the occasional light from a cottage and the flashes of lightning to see by. She had passed the last houses of the town but still had two miles to go to reach Barnessie She told herself to be patient, spoke quiet words of encouragement to Jinty, and head down against the wind, continued on her way, counting off the paces covered to herself to prevent her mind from dwelling on other thoughts.

She was almost within sight of Barnessie when she realised that Jinty was scarcely managing an amble, much less a trot. She dismounted and saw to her horror that the donkey was standing on three legs, holding the other one bent in pain. "Oh, Jinty," she moaned, "I've lamed ye in my hurry. I'm so sorry." She felt gently along the leg; she did not seem badly hurt, but riding her was out of the question. Alison sighed, almost despairing of reaching Tom in time. "Ye've got tae try," she told herself. She tied the donkey's reins to a fence by the roadside, gave her the rather wet emergency apple she kept in her pocket, and promising to come back for her as soon as she could, gathered up her sodden skirts and set off on foot towards Barnessie. In her haste she stumbled a few times, and fell to the ground once. "Keep goin', my lassie," she admonished herself, got up and turned her face resolutely towards the house.

*

Jeanie was tidying up in the kitchen, trying not to worry too much about the men out in the storm. Lady Margaret had finally managed to get a sorrowful Kate to go to bed, having promised to read to her for a while. Sir Malcolm lingered in the kitchen, talking to David.

"Here's hoping they get away a' right," he said. "I dinnae even ken if the ship'll sail in this storm."

"We just have tae hope," said David, getting to his feet. "I'll gang and check the stables meantime."

Just then they heard a feeble knocking at the door, barely audible above the noise of the storm. They exchanged worried glances. Was it the watch, come for Tom? David opened the door and discovered Alison Fleming, soaked, mud-stained and half-fainting on the threshold.

"What the devil . . .? Alison! Come in, come in. What brings ye here?"

Jeanie, appearing behind him, drew Alison towards the hearth. "In the name o' the wee man, lassie, ye're soaked through. Come tae the fire, an' I'll mak' ye a hot toddy. Ye'll catch yer death otherwise."

Alison looked round wildly. "Where's Tom?" she cried.

"They're awa' tae Dunure. They left aboot fifteen minutes since. I'm right sorry ye missed him, lassie." Jeanie tried to press Alison into a chair by the fire.

"We've got tae stop them." Alison's voice rose in panic. "I ken what happened. It's Mungo. Mungo killed Mr. Cunningham, an', oh it's terrible, he was his faither."

There was a moment's shocked silence, then Sir Malcolm said, "Ye're right, lass, we maun gang efter them. I saw Mungo was in a right queer mood, mair nor usual."

"I want tae gang wi' ye," said Alison.

"Ye will not," said Sir Malcolm, "Ye're exhausted, an' it's nae job for a lassie."

"I must," said Alison simply. For a moment they stared at each other, then Sir Malcolm sighed. "I cannae stop ye, I suppose. David, tak' Prince. He's fast and steady. He'll get ye there quickest."

David went to saddle the horse while Jeanie made Alison drink the hot whisky and sugar. "Get oot o' these wet things," she said. "I'll fetch ye some o' Bob's duds, some breeks an' a jacket. It'll be better for ridin', tae." She bustled off, while Alison did her best to contain her impatience.

She tried to tell her story to Sir Malcolm, but he stopped her. "I trust ye, lass, an' we can save the explanations till later. But did ye walk a' this way frae Ayr?"

Alison explained about Jinty, and Sir Malcolm went off to rouse one of the farm hands to go and rescue the donkey. Jeanie came back with dry clothes and Alison had just finished changing when David reappeared, his face grim.

"I've got Prince ready in the yard," he said, "but there's somethin' else. My pistol's missing frae the stables, an' some powder and shot. Mungo must hae ta'en it, he kens I keep it for vermin."

Alison blanched. "Does he mean tae use it, dae ye think?"

"Wha kens what that lad thinks? But there's nae time tae lose. Are ye sure ye want tae come?"

"Mair than ever. Thank ye for everything, Jeanie," she added, embracing her swiftly before making for the door.

Outside, she nearly changed her mind. The rain had stopped, but the wind was still howling and dark storm clouds scudded across the moonlit sky. The stallion Prince stood ready, looking huge. Alison had rarely ridden anything bigger than a donkey, and hesitated for a moment. Still, the thought of Tom in danger drove her on. David mounted and she grasped the hand he reached down to swing her up behind him. Once up, she risked a look at the ground, which seemed a long way down, and tried to ignore that and the new sensation of riding bareback in men's breeches. She held on round David's waist and laid her face against his broad back.

"Hold on," he said, and they were off.

Mungo rode along behind Tom and Bob, doing his best to keep up the pace in the face of the biting wind. Now that they were on their way he felt curiously calm. He had spent so much energy in the last week keeping up a pretence, fearing that the mask would slip, that he felt drained of emotion. He tested his feelings in his mind and decided that he could finally enter the locked part of his brain which held his memories of the previous Friday night.

He remembered going to the warehouse and climbing the stairs to the office, driven by his desire to know if Richard Cunningham was in league with the smugglers, if his employer knew about his and Tom's adventures, and what his future prospects were now that Tom seemed to be the favourite. He did not know how he would broach the subject but told himself to rely on his instincts. In the inner office he was surprised to find that Mr Cunningham had company; his wife greeted him with her habitual mocking smile.

"Ah, Mungo McGillivray," she said. "We were just talking about you. It seems you have some questions to answer."

"Questions?" stammered Mungo. He had no idea what she was talking about.

"We have been auditing the books, as you know, and there is a considerable amount of money missing. You are the clerk charged with banking our receipts, so it would seem that only you can provide an explanation."

"But . . . I ken nothing aboot ony money missing."

"Nevertheless," said Isabelle Cunningham coldly, "the fact remains that small sums have been disappearing over a period of time. Now some larger sums have gone missing. You got careless, Mr McGillivray."

"It's no' true," Mungo cried. "I ken better than tae steal. It's mair than my job's worth. Tell her it's no true, Mr Cunningham!" He turned to his employer, whose face wore an expression of helpless disappointment.

"I dinnae ken what tae think, Mungo. I trusted ye, but I cannae think how else it could hae happened."

"It seems you cannot give us a satisfactory explanation, McGillivray," went on his wife. "You leave us no choice. You will be dismissed and we will send for the Sheriff to arrest you for embezzlement."

"Mr Cunningham," said Mungo desperately, "please, ye cannae dae this."

"I'm afraid we must, Mungo. I dinnae think we hae a choice."

Mungo felt a buzzing in his ears and his vision was clouded with a red mist of fury. Without thinking he seized the paper knife from the desk and lashed out in a frenzy. When he came to his senses there was blood everywhere, the knife was still in his hand and his employer lay dead. Of Isabelle Cunningham there was no sign.

And he was my faither, *I ken that noo.*

Mungo let out a howl of anguish, which was borne away on the wind.

His inner demon, whose promptings he had given in to all too often, spoke. "*No' lang noo, Mungo, an' ye'll be free o' a' this. Ye've made yer plans; just keep a cool heid.*" He felt in his pocket for the pistol; it was primed and ready. He was sorry about Tom, for he had come to like him, but he knew there would be no peace for him, in Ayr or anywhere else on earth, if Tom did not pay the price for the death of Richard Cunningham. He looked at the tall figure riding with easy assurance ahead of him. "*Aye,*" he thought, "*ye were born wi' a silver spoon in yer gab. Ye've nae idea what life's like for the likes o' me.*" Stoking the flames of jealousy would make his task easier when the time came.

*

David and Alison, riding fast, breasted the hill above Dunure. The wild wind blew scudding clouds across the face of the moon, and whipped the waves of the Firth to a frenzy, so that David wondered how Tom would be able to make it to the ship, if it came. Alison, dazed from the ride, clung on grimly as they began the descent to the castle ruins, which stood stark and bare on the edge of the cliff.

David reined in under the castle walls and they dismounted. They could see the horses grouped restlessly nearby, but there was no other sign of life. Suddenly "What the devil...?" cried David, running towards a figure he had spotted, lying huddled at the castle entrance. It was Bob. He tried to sit up as they approached. "Somebody knocked me oot," he gasped. "It must hae been Mungo. Quick, he'll hae followed Tom inside."

David ran for the entrance, followed closely by Alison. Inside, they stumbled up the rough steps towards the great hall, slipping more than once on the wet stairs, drawn by the sound of voices. At the top David stopped at the sight of Mungo and Tom face to face, Mungo with a drawn pistol. Quickly he pushed Alison behind him, fearing that she would rush towards Tom, and stepped forward.

He realised then that Mungo was speaking. "I'm sorry, Tom, but it's a' your fault. You got me into this, poking yer nose intae the smuggling an' the company business. Could ye no' hae left weel alane? If ye hadnae come tae work at Cunningham's, nane o' this would hae happened."

"But ye already kent aboot the smuggling ..." began Tom.

"Aye, but no' that Mr Cunningham would be killed. We'll never prove it was the Kennedy gang, everybody thinks it's you so ye'll need tae bide here an' be punished. Can ye no' see? I've got tae gang awa', I've to tae get on that ship ..."

His tone was mounting as his anger grew, and David could see his finger tightening on the trigger. It was time to intervene.

"Mungo," he said mildly, "We ken wha killed Mr Cunningham."

Aware now of the presence of others, Mungo swung round.

"It was you, wasn't it? We've found the knife."

Mungo's face darkened in fury. "No, no, it wasnae me," he cried. "Ye've a' got it wrang. I never meant him ony harm, I ..."

He broke off, then suddenly turned back round towards Tom and fired. Tom fell. Mungo took off at a run through the archway towards the stairs leading to the upper floors.

"See tae Tom," yelled David, chasing hard behind Mungo. The stone steps were steep and slippery, and he stumbled more than once in his haste to get to Mungo before he had time to reload the pistol. He emerged on to the upper landing at the top of the roofless tower, where the bitter wind howled in the gaps between the stones. In the narrow space he came face to face with Mungo, who was standing by the gap where once there had been a window, trying to reload the pistol, sobbing with frustrated rage.

"Mungo," said David gently, "we've got the proof. It'll dae ye nae guid tae kill other folks. Ye'd best gi'e me the pistol noo."

Mungo looked around wildly, then all at once the will seemed to go out of him, for he lowered the pistol and moved to take a step towards David. But his feet slipped on the worn stones and he fell backwards through the gap and disappeared from view. David rushed towards the opening and looked down. Far below, Mungo lay on his back on the rocks, his body bent and his neck twisted. The moon, sailing out from behind a cloud, showed the dark pool spreading behind his head and silvered his livid face. He was obviously dead.

*

Back down in the hall, David found Alison sitting on the ground, cradling Tom's head and holding her jerkin to his shoulder in an attempt to stop the flow of blood. Tom's face was ashen and he had lost consciousness.

"He's ta'en a bullet in his arm," she wept. "There's a' this blood..."

"Here," said David, stripping off his jacket and shirt. "Tear strips off the shirt an' tie it roon' the top o' his arm, as tight as ye can. Whaur's Bob?"

"He's gone tae the village for help. Mungo?"

"He fell frae the tower." Davey grimaced. "He's beyond help."

Alison swallowed, then nodded. "Maybe it's better so. But his puir mither."

*

Bob came back from Dunure village with the blacksmith and his horse and cart. They loaded Tom on to the cart and Alison sat with him, tying and retying the strips of shirt to staunch the bleeding. It was agreed that they would return for Mungo's body the next day, when the tide had gone out and the wind had died down. The sorry little procession left Dunure and the Dublin-bound ship, which had put out in the storm and waited in vain for a signal, went on its way.

During the night the relentless waves loosened the broken body of Mungo McGillivray from the rocks and as the tide turned the currents carried it far away from Carrick shore.

EPILOGUE

SEPTEMBER 28th

The piper and the two fiddlers struck the final chord of the eightsome reel with a flourish, wiped their brows and stowed their instruments beneath the chairs before going in search of their interval refreshment. They went straight to the head of the queue for the punch bowl, ignoring the good-natured jeers of those waiting behind them.

"Weel played, lads," said Jeanie Balfour as she ladled punch into their cups. "Ye've earned yer supper."

"What's in the punch, mistress?" asked the piper.

"It's my man's secret recipe," beamed Jeanie, indicating Bob who was replenishing the bowl, "but I'll wager ye'll no' be disappointed. Forbye, James Cunningham's no' here tae disapprove." Appreciative laughter followed her as she went off to fetch the pies.

The first ball of the season was in full swing at the Assembly Rooms. The hall was crowded, for it seemed that all of Ayr society was there, with the exception of the Cunningham brothers. "Puir Mr Richard," as he was generally referred to now, was of course no more, and his brother James had disappeared from the town before his case came before the Kirk Session. This was taken as a sure sign of guilt and if all the rumours were to be believed he had forced his attentions on half the women of the town.

Tom, standing by a pillar at the side of the room, looked round fondly at the company as they strolled and chatted under the bright lights. The Misses McFadzean were seated near the door, surveying the comings and goings with avid interest. Miss Effie was dressed in pale pink satin and her sister in pale blue; both sported the high powdered hairstyles and face patches they hoped were the latest Edinburgh fashion. The overall effect remained mutton dressed as lamb, but the colours were less strident than usual. Perhaps Alison's influence was bearing fruit.

Over near the musicians David was in earnest conversation with Rab Burns. Tom was sure that the topic would be the dreadful weather and the late harvest, judging by the seriousness of David's expression and Rab's monosyllabic answers as his eye was caught by a succession of comely lassies. As soon as the music started again, he would be off.

Tom himself would not be dancing. His arm had almost healed but he was not yet up to stripping the willow. He still counted himself lucky every day to be alive, free and with his family, but it was hard to come to terms with the fact that Mungo had killed Richard Cunningham and nearly killed him too. The discovery of the knife and Isabelle Cunningham's testimony had clearly established Mungo's guilt and secured Tom's immediate freedom, but there were still those who muttered that Tom Boyd was fortunate to have a wealthy, privileged family to protect him.

There were few in Ayr to mourn Mungo McGillivray, and no-one seemed minded to look for his mother. Annie had disappeared too. It was said that she had completely lost her wits and was living in a cave on the shore somewhere down near Girvan; she had been seen begging in that town.

Kate had taken Mungo's death hard. She had lost her first grown-up friend and could not understand how someone who had been so kind to her had tried to kill her brother. She had moped around the house for days until Tom had sought her out in the walled garden, where she sat on the swing, moodily kicking at the windfall apples which strewed the grass.

"Mungo was my friend too," he'd said. "It's all right tae grieve for him; I do."

"But he was bad. He killed Mr Cunningham and he shot you."

"Weel," Tom grinned ruefully, "at least he missed me. An' if I'm right, he didnae mean tae kill Mr Cunningham. He was in a rage. Mungo wasnae a bad man at heart, an' he was fond o' you, wee sister. In a way, the last week o' his life was one o' the happiest, thanks tae you an' David."

The tears that Kate had held in check for many long days came then, and Tom held her close until at length she gulped and said quietly, "I'll aye mourn him, I think, in some part o' me, but I'm better noo." She sniffed, gave him a tearful smile, and they set off back towards the house.

A stir in the doorway brought Tom's thoughts back to the present. Some latecomers had arrived and he was surprised to see that the party included Isabelle Cunningham, on the arm of a tall man who looked vaguely familiar. The Misses McFadzean fluttered their fans furiously and muttered to each other at the sight of a woman who was supposed to be still in mourning for her husband. Isabelle was no longer in black but her sober grey silk dress enhanced rather than disguised her proud beauty as her glance swept the room, defying gossip.

Seeing Tom, she whispered something to her companion, who went off towards the refreshment table while Isabelle approached Tom, smiling a greeting.

"Monsieur Tom. You are quite recovered, I see."

"Almost. My arm is nearly healed. How are you, Madam?"

"I am well, as you see."

"And the business? I dinnae see Mr Kennedy here the nicht."

"Adam Kennedy is no longer in my employ," answered Mrs Cunningham smoothly. "Nor are certain of his associates. I had long suspected that they were not entirely honest, and I had to dismiss them. I believe they intend to go to the colonies."

Tom was surprised. The last time he had seen Isabelle he had assumed that Kennedy was her lover. Seeing his look, Isabelle drew closer.

"*Le commerce*, Tom," she murmured. "*Le commerce avant*

tout. You have not asked me if *you* are still a Cunningham employee."

"I assumed I was not. But ..."

"Do not worry. I am sure you have no desire to come back to Cunningham's, nor do I expect it of you." She smiled and touched his arm.

"You saved my life," said Tom. "I am in your debt."

"Yes," she said softly. "You would do well to remember that." Just for a moment Tom caught a glimpse of something cold and hard in her eyes which made him shiver, but then she laughed and turned to the tall man who was approaching, bearing glasses of punch, so that he wondered if he had imagined it.

"May I introduce my new business associate, Gavin McKie," she said, accepting her glass.

"We've met," said McKie with an easy smile. "I trust ye're weel, Mr Boyd." Tom recognised the excise officer who had inspected Cunningham's back in August. He wondered just what "business associate" meant.

"Quite weel, I thank ye."

After a few polite exchanges, Tom excused himself and went to ponder these new revelations. It seemed that Isabelle Cunningham had quite recovered from the loss of her husband and now meant to run the business she had inherited her way. Tom reflected bitterly on how different things would have been if Richard Cunningham had recognised Mungo as his son. He had given him a job, but nothing more, and he had never told his wife about their connection. He shook his head to clear it of these melancholy, useless thoughts and went to join his family.

"There ye are," said Sir Malcolm, "I thocht yon merry widow was gonnae eat ye. Did she want tae gi'e ye yer job back?"

Tom shook his head. "No. I couldnae gang back there onyway."

"Aye, it's for the best. So, what will ye dae noo?"

"I dinnae ken, faither. The law, maybe." He looked hopefully at his father.

"I doot they'll want a jailbird like yersel'," opined Sir Malcolm. "My influence doesnae stretch that far." But his tone was kind.

"So what dae ye suggest?"

His father smiled in a mysterious way that reminded Tom fleetingly of Isabelle Cunningham.

"I've got an idea, but I'll no' tell ye yet. Get yer strength back first. There's time enough."

"Aye," said David, who had overheard. "A few weeks helpin' us get this harvest in an' the ploughin' done will set ye up fine."

Tom groaned.

"Meantime," said his mother as the band started up again, "even if ye cannae dance yet there's a young lassie ower there that ye've been neglecting. Come on, my dear," she added, turning to her husband, "it's time for us tae tak' a turn on the floor."

With a lighter heart, Tom went over to where Alison sat with her father. Greetings over, "Mistress Fleming," he said, "as my arm hasnae quite healed, may I have the pleasure of sitting out this dance wi' ye?"

"Of course." Alison smiled and made room for him beside her on the bench. Her father grunted and moved aside a little.

"How are ye keepin', Tom?" she asked. "Ye say your arm's no' quite healed. It's been near a month noo."

"it's a lot better, but I cannae lift onything heavy yet. David says that's just an excuse for no' helping on the farm. The doctor says I'll make a full recovery though, thanks tae you."

"No' just me." Alison fell silent, thinking back to the events of that awful night.

"But if ye hadnae been tae Annie's then ridden through the storm tae fetch help, I wouldnae be here."

"I couldnae hae done onything withoot David and Bob, and yer faither makin' us ride Prince." Alison shuddered. "Yon's a fine beast, but I'm in nae hurry tae ride him again. Jinty'll dae me fine."

"A brave wee donkey. She played her part an' a."

"Since we're talkin' aboot it . . ." began Alison.

"What is it, lass?"

"Is there ony news o' Mungo? I mean, did they find him?"

"Nae sign onywhere. I dinnae suppose there will be noo. Annie's disappeared as weel, they say."

Alison sighed. "I'm heartsore aboot Annie. I've been tae the hoose a few times, but it's cauld an' bare. The lads frae the brewery hae been an' lifted the few wee things she had. I'm aye wonderin' what's become o' her."

"They say she's been seen doon by Girvan, begging. I think she might be livin' in one o' the caves on the shore. I ken some folk do."

"Tom . . ." she hesitated.

"Ye want tae gang an' find her."

"I couldnae rest easy if I didnae at least try. Would ye . . ."

"Come wi' ye? Of course I will. We'll gang the morn, if ye like."

"Could we? Oh Tom, thank you." She grasped his arm, making him wince. "Oh, I'm sorry."

Tom merely grinned and moved a little closer on the bench. They turned to look at the dance floor, where Sir Malcolm and Lady Margaret were leading a set in a stately strathspey.

"Your parents are looking well."

"Aye. My mither's got a braw new gown. She must hae a new dressmaker, no' yon optician's nightmare frae the Sandgate."

"Tom Boyd, ye ken fine I made her gown. An' if ye look at yer aunties, ye can see they've changed their colours an' a."

"Weel, they're a bit mair pastel, I'll gie ye that, an' I suppose ye didnae hae ony say in the hairstyles."

Alison made to punch his arm but remembered not to just in time.

"What will ye dae noo, Tom?" she asked.

"My faither's got somethin' in mind but he's no' tellin' me just yet, so you could say I've got a wee holiday. I'm planning a trip tae the shore the morn wi' a young lady, an' then I was gonnae ask her faither if he'd let me court her, if she's willin' of course." Tom looked into Alison's shining eyes and read his answer there.

"Faither," she said, "what dae ye say tae that?"

Mr Fleming, busy relighting his pipe, studied Tom over its bowl for a long moment, then grunted, "Aye. Ye'll dae."

"Dinnae mind him, Tom. That's high praise."

They smiled at each other and, under her shawl, Tom found and held her hand.

*

Isabelle Cunningham sat in her chair at the desk in what was now her office, working on the company's accounts. The desk had been her husband's, but she had changed the rug and the chair, although the room held no terrors for her. She did not believe in ghosts.

She allowed herself a small sigh of satisfaction. The business was flourishing with new personnel and her hands firmly on the reins. The presence of Gavin McKie lent it an air of honest legitimacy and he would not interfere with her plans; she would see to that. She reflected that things had turned out very well – Tom Boyd was in her debt and Mungo, her pawn, was no more. With a complacent smile she sipped from her cup of chocolate and continued her task of restoring the figures she had altered to their original values.

*

The midday sun, stealing into the cave, played upon the face of the red-haired woman. She woke, groaning, and heaved herself upright, trying to bring some movement into her numb and weary limbs. The effort exhausted her and she sat for some moments, fighting for breath. Finally she hauled herself to her feet and looked around for the bottle. It was there, but it was empty. Cursing, she threw it across the cave to smash on the rocks and staggered towards the cave mouth.

Outside, the sun was bright and the breeze kind, and the salty sea air revived her a little. She stumbled over sharp rocks to the water's edge and looked out, as she did every day, over the shining silvery waters towards the great blue-grey Craig. She stood there motionless for a long time, her eyes searching the empty sea.

A shout from along the shore caught her attention and she thought she heard someone calling her name. She turned slowly. A man and a woman were scrambling over the rocks towards her. She fancied she recognised the woman, but it meant nothing to her. Turning back to the sea she called her son's name, as she did every day, but her voice was drowned by the cries of the gulls and the endless waves beating on the shore.